THE CHOICE

By

Anne Greene

Published by Forget Me Not Romances, a Division Of Winged Publications.

THE CHOICE
Copyright © 2019 by Anne Greene

Editor: Cynthia Hickey
Book Design by Forget Me Not Romances

All rights reserved. No part of this publication may be reproduced, stored in a retrieval system, or transmitted in any form or by any means—electronic, mechanical, photocopying, recording, or otherwise—without the prior written permission of the publisher. The only exception is brief quotations in printed reviews. Piracy is illegal. Thank you for respecting the hard work of this author.

This book is a work of fiction. Names, characters, Places, incidents, and dialogues are either products of the author's imagination or used fictitiously.
Any resemblance to actual persons, living or dead, or events is coincidental. Scripture quotations from The Authorized (King James) Version.

ISBN-13: 9798604761588

DEDICATION

I dedicate this book to every reader who has ever fallen in love.

As ever, I dedicate this book to my supportive husband, Colonel Larry Greene.

Above all, I dedicate this book to my Lord and Savior, Jesus Christ

Ephesians 3:20-21 – Now unto Him that is able to do exceeding abundantly above all that we ask or think, according to the power that worketh in us, unto Him be glory in the church by Christ Jesus throughout all ages, world without end. KJV – **Felicity's Verse.**

I Corinthians 15:58 – Therefore, my beloved brethren, be ye steadfast, unmovable, always abounding in the work of the Lord, forasmuch as ye know that your labor is not in vain in the Lord. KJV – **Ben's Verse.**

CHAPTER 1

Laramie (in what would become Wyoming) - 1850

"If I wanted to stay single, I'd wait for the perfect man." As she carried the wooden sign toward the large storefront window of Ft. Laramie's only general store, Felicity Daniels' long, pink gingham skirts brushed the floor.

She passed between the barrels of flour and boxes of food clustered on the wooden-plank-floor and the shelves stacked high with dry goods.

Papa's old friend, Jedidiah Adams, planted a hand on her arm and stopped her rush. "Now, jist take some time and think this through."

"I don't have any more time." Felicity gently removed his hand and wended on through the piled-high goods to the front of McVey's General Store. She stared out the huge front window for a second, then bent and pushed several bolts of flannel yard goods out of the way. She shook her head. "No, this is better." And positioned the material so the heavy denim and calico bolts held up her sign.

WANTED: GROOM BETWEEN THE AGES OF 20 AND 30. STRONG, ABLE-BODIED WITH NO DISFIGUREMENT. CHRISTIAN. EAGER TO TRAVEL TO THE OREGON TERRITORY. ALL EXPENSES PAID. APPLY INSIDE. FELICITY DANIELS.

She straightened and set her jaw.

She'd given Ben many chances to fall in love with her during the two months she'd been stranded in Ft. Laramie. She'd had no success, and time had run out. Ben ignored every one of her not at all subtle hints. Even said *no* to her offer to take him for a buggy ride and a picnic. She stood, hands on her hips gazing at her handiwork. "Since it's essential I get married, rather than the perfect man, I'll settle for a good one."

"You could keep on clerkin' here at the gen'l store." Jed stroked his flowing silver mustache.

"That's not an option, Jedediah. Mr. McVey specified this would only be a temporary job until the last wagon train departs and business falls off. The last travelers leave in two days. I mean to go with them."

Jed lumbered to join her at the window. "Even unmarried settlers can claim three hundred twenty acres of that free land in the Oregon Territory.

That should be enough land for you." Jedediah placed a heavy hand on her shoulder. "I know. I know. To get the whole six hundred forty acres you gotta have yourself a husband. I'd apply for the job myself, but ain't nobody gonna believe I'm yer husband. Good-looking young gal like you." He blew out a breath. "You best settle for the smaller tract of land. Good husbands don't grow on trees."

"According to *The Donation Land Claim Act,* the authorities won't allow a lone woman to claim that free land." Felicity flipped her long, blonde braid over her shoulder. "Besides, how do you suppose I can stake my claim on that land, cut down trees, build a house and a barn, and plant those acres all by myself?" She tossed her head, swirling her long blonde braid from her back to her shoulder. "I need a man with a strong back and big muscles. If he knows how to string a sentence together so much the better."

"I'm bound to take care of you myself, even with my rheumatism makin' me hobble like an old geezer." Jed gripped her arm. "Why are you so bent on leaving here? Not two months back, yer daddy's dying words asked me to take care of you." He jutted a white-whiskered jaw. "And that's exactly what I aim to do. Right here in Ft. Laramie. I'm not lettin' my life-long friend down. We was like brothers."

Felicity gave Papa's old friend a gentle smile. "Papa and I set out for the Willamette Valley in that Oregon Territory to forge our destiny in a new land." She tugged her arm free. "We've traveled this far to that Promised Land, and I don't plan to be stuck here in the middle of nowhere when I have two perfectly fine prairie schooners still loaded with provisions and the mules to pull them. Those mules are eating me out of Papa's savings. I can't afford to stay here any longer."

"Now, Felly, don't go off like a hog gone wild. Let's think this through." Jed shook his head until his silver mustache trembled.

She stared Jed down. "I'm out of time. I'm through thinking. It's time to act. The last wagon train of the year leaves in two days. Any later trains will get caught by winter. I've got to travel now." She strode to the front door and pushed one of the double doors open.

The bell above the door chimed. Gathering her skirts, she stepped outside into the late August heat.

Jed hobbled through the door and stood by her on the uneven boardwalk. "That's some sign you painted. But I told you, won't do no good to drive a man yer fixin' to corral. Jus' leave yer gate open a crack and let 'em bust in."

"I left my gate open wide with one man. Didn't work. I don't have any more time for those shenanigans. Two days from now, I leave." She glanced up and down the busy boardwalk. "And I've got to have a groom." Stepping back, she admired her hand-printed sign. The white paint on dark wood showed up well, blasting her message to the people bustling by.

"What mule-headed man will answer a sign like that? He'd have to be at the end of his rope to marry-up with you jist to get six hundred forty acres in the Oregon Territory."

"Are you saying a man would be crazy to marry me?" Felicity puckered her forehead and glared.

"Now, now, don't get yer dander up." Jed rubbed a weathered hand on the back of his wrinkled neck and his face sagged. "Yer so purty you look more ornamental than useful. How's that man to know what a strong, capable woman you are?"

"He had two months to find out. He's lost his chance. When the right man applies, I'll know him." She wrung her hands together as if washing Ben right out of them. "I've prayed about this, and God hasn't brought any other solution to my mind." She moved aside so passersby could see her sign. "What's marriage anyway, but two people building a new life together and establishing a home site on wonderful, fertile land? The land I'm sure of, and I'm trusting God will bring the right man."

"Them flyers you put such store by promise green, rolling hills, fenced land, herds of contented cattle, and flourishing crops." Jed swiped a work-hardened veined hand across his mouth. "Mabbe they're pie in the sky and promise more than they give. Ever think of that?"

She smiled as images flashed through her mind of permanence, stability, peace. How she yearned for a home of her own.

The wooden sidewalk vibrated under passing feet.

Farmers with broad shoulders and their big-hipped wives with unsmiling lips, their sun-bonneted heads turned back toward their three or four children, plodded by. Cowboys with guns strapped on their hips and tall hats with large brims dipped low on their foreheads tromped by as if they owned the fort. A few soldiers, their blue uniforms making them appear taller and broader than they were, glanced at her. Several children rolled hoops down the busy street. Wagons raised dust on the road, stirring up the odor of old manure. Everyone who trudged by gaped at her sign. No one turned into the store.

Shouts of team masters and the bustle of wagons wafted over the stockade wall behind the store, coming from the pastures outside.

"Wagon train is fixing to resume its long journey. No way you can find a suitable husband afore they leave." Jeb shook his head, so his silver hair stood out like spokes from a wheel.

Felicity pulled in a deep breath. Oh, the familiar noise brought an ache. She and Papa started out in early April, and they got just one-third of the way before they got stopped here at Ft. Laramie. She'd never forget when the cholera hit Papa. Though she'd done her best to nurse him, he'd not lasted a week. A shiver crept down her spine. If only she could forget Papa's sunken eyes and the clammy texture of his skin as he gripped her hand. He'd been a tall, hardy, healthy man, her strength and the rock of her existence. Nothing seemed impossible for him. As he died, he made her promise to go on to the new land and create a fresh start. But he'd died before he could tell her the reasons why they raced from Independence, Missouri, in such a hurry. Running as if someone chased them.

No matter, she had her suspicions. During the whole journey here, Papa had looked over his shoulder. With Papa's last breath, he'd begged her to get married. He'd said he had many good reasons why she needed to change her last name.

So, she'd promised him.

Nothing in this raw fort town beckoned her to stay. Even without her promise, she longed to leave. When the wagon train moved out there'd be little left here, but the general store and the small fortification garrisoned with twenty or thirty soldiers. No women lingered behind except Sal, running her boarding house, and a couple Indian women who did laundry for the soldiers. All humanity plunged onward to grab a piece of that free land. If she waited until the wagons rolled again next year, the free land would be taken. She'd be too late.

"Well, Felly, when a woman starts draggin' a loop, there's always some man willin' to step into it."

She nodded. "God will send the

right man. I hope you're praying with me that he arrives in time and applies." No use wishing her groom had those unforgettable eyes as blue as the sky on a clear summer day. God hadn't answered that prayer.

"I'm a praying you'll change that stubborn mind of yours." Jed patted her shoulder.

"That's not going to happen." Felicity took Jed's hand and gazed into his grey eyes, still lively in their bed of wrinkles. White hair from his bushy brows drifted down over his drooping lids. "You're a godly man, please pray God will send a believing man to help me on my way." She squeezed his fingers. "Wouldn't hurt if he were good to look at."

"Felicity, honey, don't get your hopes high. When yer daddy and I started this pilgrimage together, we both thought we was younger than we turned out to be. But whatever happens, I can't let you go alone. I might be a hindrance, but I'm comin' with ya."

Jed's slow-talking words flew straight to her heart.

She pulled him by the hand back inside the slightly cooler general store. Throwing her arms around his burly body, she hugged with all her strength. "Thank you so very much, Jed. I love all that beauty inside you. But I don't want to take you beyond what your strength can handle. If anything happened to you, I would never forgive myself."

"Don't you worry none, Felly. There're good years left in this old frame. I might slow you down a tad, but God knows that would probably be best. I'm thinkin' yer goin' off faster than a cat with her tail on fire."

"Just pray, Jed. Just pray for the right man to come inside and apply."

The above-the-door bell jangled. A few men entered, darted glances around the store and then headed toward the back counter. Four more men entered. Then the wood floor trembled under countless boots. A stream of men pushing and shoving boiled into the store.

Her mouth dropped open. She let Jed go and scurried behind the store counter. Good heavens, was it a stampede?

Jed lumbered up beside her and dropped both fists on the counter. "Felly, I'm thinkin' you best charge each man who wants to take you up on yer offer ten dollars apiece jist to apply." The overhead lantern flashed his white hair silver as he nodded. "Or you'll never make headway through this mob."

Men continued to spill into the store and lined up three deep at the counter. The line stretched out the open door and down the sidewalk.

Had she bitten off too big a bite? Oh, if only one of God's Christmas Angels would step in to help. She really needed a husband for Christmas.

Jed emptied a number of one-pound sacks of kidney beans from a basket and slid the woven container over in front of her. He pushed a child's school slate over and handed her a piece of chalk. "Ten dollars each."

"That's a week's wage. Don't you think—?"

"Yep, thet's fair!" Jed climbed up on an overturned wooden box and waved his flannel-coated arms. "Gents, are ye here cause of the sign in the winder?"

Deep throated, tenor, bass, and baritone voices chorused, "Yes!"

"Well, if ye wants to talk with the little lady, ye gots to drop ten dollars in the basket."

Silence for the barest moment, then pushing and shoving men burst forward to thrust a ten-dollar gold piece into the basket.

Felicity gaped. Gold dollars!

"Gold's easier to come by than

silver these days. Money's flooding out of California territory, thanks to the gold rush," Jed whispered. "Shut yer mouth and start takin' names."

Felicity blinked. A few seconds passed before she gained her senses. "Stop! Stop!" She gazed at the assorted well-dressed and the motley-clothed crew of men churning in front of the store counter. "I...I won't take your money unless I think you might be a likely candidate. So, please stop tossing money in my basket and form a line. If I think you might be considered, you may deposit your ten-dollar gold piece, and I'll write your name on my list."

She pushed up the fitted sleeves of her pink-gingham dress, took the chalk, and gazed at the man standing first in line. Too slender. She needed muscle. "I'm so sorry, but I'm afraid you won't do. If you gave me a gold piece, please retrieve your money from the basket."

Jed nodded and pushed the basket toward the man.

"Aw, girlie. I need me a missus so I can get an extra three hundred twenty acres. I'll even pay my own way. I just need a wife."

Felicity tossed her head and winked at Jed. Ha! These men wanted a wife for the same reason she required a husband. Beneath her long skirts she tapped a jig with suddenly lighter feet. These men knew exactly what they signed up for.

"You heard Miss Daniels. Next." Jed's deep voice carried the authority he'd used as the foremost blacksmith in Independence, Missouri, before he retired. Many a teamster had quaked at that tone.

The twiggy man fumbled in the basket, his thin fingers closed over a gold piece, and he turned and shuffled out, his mouth pulled down at the corners.

As the next man in line stepped

forward, his pungent odor preceded him. Perhaps he'd just arrived and hadn't had time to go to the hotel for a bath. No, several days ago he'd come into the store to buy flour and a new pair of boots. He'd been in Ft. Laramie long enough to clean up. "I'm sorry. Please take your money."

The man frowned and raised a fist.

Jed cleared his throat.

The man lowered his head, dug into the money basket, and retrieved his gold piece.

Felicity gazed at the next man. Clean. Tall. Muscles. Not too old. "You may leave your application fee. Please spell your name, and I'll write it on the slate." She poised the chalk.

He tipped his big hat, spelled his name, and gave her a pleasant smile.

His nose was large, but he had an agreeable look about him. "Next."

Another four men passed her initial exam, and she wrote their names on the slate.

Oh, dear heavenly Father, please send the right man. Seems quite a few men want a wife as well as have their way paid to the Oregon Territory. How shall I ever find the right groom?

All afternoon men either passed or failed her first look. None stood out in her mind. Some wore denims and chambray shirts, some wore cowhide chaps and wool vests and carried leather gauntlets, and a few wore store-bought suits. All wore six-shooters strapped to their hips and carried big hats in work-hardened hands.

Soon all the men looked the same. Was every single man in town lining up in front of the counter? She sighed. "Jed, please use another chalkboard and add that the man must be a Christian who regularly attends church. I'm sure that will cut the list down. I should have thought of that at once."

After Jed added the words and held up the sign, a few men frowned, left the line, and stomped out. Several others sauntered out of the store as if they hadn't wanted to apply after all. One man grabbed a gold coin from the basket, dipped his chin, and slunk out the door.

But a good many men stayed.

Those men whose names she'd written on the chalkboard loitered around the store, sitting on barrels, standing braced against the wall, leaning over the counter, or squatting on the floor waiting to see what she required next.

"Oh, dear. What shall I do now? I never thought I'd have more than one or two men who would accept my offer." Her ankle-high laced boots pinched her feet. Her head pounded. How could she find the right man in this horde? Her petticoat stuck to her drawers in the heat of so many bodies. The stays, usually so comfortable, poked her ribs. "There must be twenty men waiting for me to interview them."

"Well, missy, you'll just have to add some more qualifications." Jed slid another small chalkboard down the counter to her.

Felicity gazed at the gang of men scattered around the store. Some tried to appear unconcerned, others looked anxious, and many wore a stony expression to hide their thoughts. She didn't want to live in close quarters with a stranger for four more months, and the more she thought of her scheme, the more she felt like a fool. But she and Papa had faced too many hardships to get this far. She couldn't stop now.

Allowing a man to drive one of her wagons and eat at her campfire would be another affliction she had to face. She knew how to put her shoulder to the wheel and keep on plodding when the going got rough. Hadn't she done that all her life? And the fact that these men pursued a wife for the same reason she hunted for a husband made her deal a lot sweeter. She had a clear conscience.

She promised Papa she would start a new life in the Oregon Territory ... so she would. She'd promised him she would marry ... so she would.

"If any of you men smoke or chew, please take your gold piece out of the basket. I won't marry a man who smokes." She wrote the new demands on the chalkboard.

Two men glowered at her and reached for their ten dollars.

"I won't marry a man who drinks." She chalked that onto her requirement list.

A lanky cowboy's hand shot up. "Um, Ma'am, do you mean drink just a little now and again, or do you mean get drunk?"

"I mean, I don't want a man who drinks even one small drink of hard liquor at the end of a trail ride. I mean, no drinking at all."

Grumbling, more men moved toward the door. When the door shut on the last one, and the store grew quiet, half the men had taken their money and left.

Felicity pulled in a deep breath. Better. She sauntered out from behind the counter and zigzagged among the remaining men. All strong and healthy-looking. All tall. All passed the smell test. As she swished by each one, the man produced his best smile. All pleasant looking.

She gazed at Jed and shrugged. "I'd prefer a man who is intelligent. Who can carry on a conversation."

"You want a man who can be plenty smart without strugglin' to make a job out of it." Jed shook his head. "Maybe you should write them up a quiz. You were the Assistant Editor of the *Independence Times*. You know how to do thet."

As she hurried over to Jed, Felicity's high-laced shoes tapped the floor. She whispered, "I think it best you don't mention my job or my father as editor. He wanted to keep that information quiet."

Jed bobbed his head, his long hair swinging in his face.

"O.K. men, I'm going to dine at the hotel. I'll meet those of you who are still interested in the job back here in two hours. In the meantime, please consider why you are qualified to handle this position and be prepared to state your case." She held out her arm to Jed and the two of them made their way through the general store and out onto the street.

The hot evening still held some daylight, though most folks had gone to their supper, leaving the sidewalk less crowded.

"Oh, I never expected such a response." Felicity tried not to frown. Seemed every man in Ft. Laramie wanted to marry her … except the one man she'd prayed would apply. Why hadn't he? From the looks of his worn boots, Ben didn't appear to be rolling in money.

The boardwalk still vibrated with footsteps, but the farm families who would depart with the wagon train had returned to their camps. Wood smoke, with mouth-watering scents of beef cooking over spits and coffee boiling, wafted over the high pickets surrounding the small fort. She motioned in that direction. "I loved those meals by the campfires after a long day of driving the mules or walking beside the covered wagons."

"Seems purty sure you will again. You and me took turns driving one wagon, and your papa drove the other. Reckon your new husband will drive the other wagon now."

She blinked against tears that *would* prickle her eyes and demand to fall. She and Papa had loved sitting by the fire and listening to cowboys' harmonicas and singing hymns before they crawled into their bedrolls. "How can I possibly go on without Papa?"

"Now, honey, you got something started that'd be hard to stop. Don't you fret about yer daddy. We'll find us the right fella." Jed put his gnarled fist under her chin and tilted her head up. "And you don't have to marry him. You and me will sign up for my three hundred twenty acres. See if we don't."

"But Papa wanted six hundred and forty acres. He'd sent our man, Jabez, to scout out the land. Jabez sent word that to be profitable, a man needed all six hundred forty acres."

"And then that slave never came back, did he?"

Felicity shook her head. "He would have been such a help on this trip. But Papa pretty much thought Jabez would take off once he reached the Oregon Territory." She smiled. "Land's not the only commodity free out west. At least Jabez sent back his report."

"Thet slave wouldn't have solved your problem. But he would have been a big help workin' thet land."

Just as the dinner bell rang, she and Jed climbed the wooden steps to the porch and walked through the front door into Sal's Boarding House.

"Say, what about that feller who's staying in the downstairs corner bedroom? I've been studyin' him, and he seems like a good, Christian man. I see him at church every Sunday."

She frowned. "I don't know. There's something about him that irritates me every time I see him." And why not? Ben had not so much as walked her to the new church after she'd dropped a wagonload of hints. Those sky-blue eyes barely acknowledged her when he breezed into the general store to buy provisions. Ben hadn't even gotten excited when she dropped everything dear Mrs. Baxter ordered into a jumbled pile in front of the sweet lady and rushed to wait on him.

But he'd gotten plenty animated choosing which goldmining pan he wanted. He'd chosen one of each. She sighed. He hadn't picked up on her hint of the picnic lunch, the carriage ride, or the pie auction. She'd spent all her spare time baking that pie. Ben had no interest in her.

"The feller's tall. He's so clean and brown, looks like he's been scrubbed with saddle soap. But you ask him where he's from and where he's aheadin', he turns as dangerous as being up a creek with a grizzly. Otherwise, he's right smart to talk with."

"Perhaps that's why I don't like him." Or more likely because he ignored her smiles and attempts at revealing her interest.

"But jist take another look. He favors one of them men in a mail-order catalog."

"Oh, he's handsome all right, with

that dark, wavy hair and those brooding blue eyes. But he gives the impression he's not interested in land in the Oregon Territory. He's got Gold Rush Fever."

What a happy day for her *if* she *could* order a man out of the catalog. A mail-order groom. That's what she needed. One who fit all her criteria. She could check off all the things she wanted in a man ... and mail him back if he didn't suit her needs. She thinned her lips. Darn if she wouldn't order one who looked just like Benjamin.

She and Jed entered the dining room. Every chair at the double-trestle table held someone except for three empty seats at the far end. Jed seated her and hunkered down across from her, leaving the chair at the end for whoever came in late.

She glanced around the table. Of course, the missing boarder had to be the dark-haired cowboy. "Do you recall his name?" She'd already gone so far as to embroider his name on her pillow slips. Well, Papa always said *'Dreams never amount to much. Just get your hopes high until someone comes along and stomps them into the ground.'* Still a blue-embroidered *BEN* on her pillow winked at her each night before she closed her eyes.

"Ben Bonneville. Cain't think why I didn't mention him to you as a possible. Seems to me he fits the bill, unless he's on the dodge from the law." Jed glanced over his shoulder at the door. "Here he comes. Now don't you go acting as prim as a preacher's wife at a prayer meetin'. I'm thinkin' this Benjamin might be jist the man we're alookin' fer."

Her cheeks heated. Too bad Ben didn't think so.

CHAPTER 2

"Evening, Mr. Bonneville." Felicity hid her irritation and tacked on her sweetest smile.

A crease formed between Ben's dark brows. His azure-blue eyes clouded like a dreary day in winter. "Evening, Miss Daniels, Jed." He tossed his big hat to the peg above the back door and hitched up the chair at the end of the table.

The landlady, Sally Thomas, presided at the head of the two long trestle tables set end to end and bowed her head. All the men, women, and children sitting at the table lowered their heads and closed their eyes.

"Lord, we thank You for the food we are about to partake of and pray You will bless it to our bodies and our bodies to Your service. In Jesus name, Amen."

Amens ranged up and down the table.

Felicity placed her napkin in her lap and gazed at the storm cloud that was Ben Bonneville. "Did you have a bad day, sir?"

"You could say that." He seized a plate of roast beef from the woman at his right and stabbed a slice of meat. "I'd say just about the worst day of my life." He thrust the serving dish to Felicity without looking up from his plate.

What awful manners. Even when grieving Papa's death, she'd tried her best to be civil to people. Her heart had ached so, she'd thought she'd never recover.

"What's the trouble, Ben?" Jed laid a hand on Ben's shoulder.

Jed's soothing voice had helped her through her worst days. Perhaps he could cheer Mr. Bonneville. She smiled at Letty, the lady at Ben's right who passed him the mashed potatoes.

Ben shook his dark head. Bristles shadowed his tan skin as if he hadn't taken time to shave today. "Don't want to bother you folks with my troubles." He glared at her.

Her heart fluttered at that deep-blue gaze. Drat! She'd abandoned hope about Mr. Ben Bonneville. If only the butterflies in her stomach would lose heart as well.

"I heard palaver that some silly woman put a sign up in the general store. Can't think any woman in this male dominated country would be so hard up she had to advertise for a husband."

Felicity lifted her chest, stiffened her back, and tossed her braid over her shoulder. "That is my sign, sir." Her tone could have iced a gallon of sweet tea.

Ben swallowed and choked on the meat. He coughed. His face reddened. "Seems I stuck my boot into my mouth there." He grabbed a drink of water.

"Yep. You did." Jed forked a slab of beef. "Maybe you could tell us what made yer day so bad."

As if he'd lost his appetite, Ben slid his plate, stacked high with food, toward the center of the table and wiped his mouth on his napkin. "Might as well. Maybe save you folks from my fate." He gulped another drink of water, leaned forward, and raised his voice. "I've been robbed." He waved his hands over his blue plaid shirt. "All I have left are the clothes on my back. The thief stripped me of everything else I own."

Felicity gasped. "I'm so sorry."

A murmur ran up and down the table.

"I've got two bits in my pocket between me and starvation." Ben's mouth hung down at the corners.

Questions flew up and down the dining table. Everyone gaped at him.

"Yep. My horse, Salvation's, missing from the stable, too. I got nothing left."

"Seems like you might want to add your name to Felicity's list of prospective husbands." Jed forked some green beans into his mouth and winked.

Felicity's face heated. If only she could slide down under the table. She smacked Jed's free hand lying on the wooden tabletop.

"Well, that sounds like a mighty fine offer for some lucky gent." Ben coughed. "But a wife doesn't fit anywhere into my plans."

"And why not?" Jed's eyes widened like he was as wise as a tree full of owls.

"Not that it's any of your business,

but before she died my mother racked up quite a debt with expensive medical bills. I'm obliged to pay them. I'm off to join the gold rush."

"Sounds like an honorable thing to do. But cain't you earn thet money just as well on the acreage Felicity's going to get in Oregon? Might take a bit longer until harvest time. Her way is slower but sure as shootin' surer." Jed sipped his coffee, his eyes staring Ben down, his silver mustache glowing in the candlelight.

"That might be so, but I've heard God's call. When I reach those gold rush towns, I'm going to ride circuit and preach to those miners and prospectors." He rubbed the muscles at the back of his neck and frowned as if he had a massive headache. "And I've never heard of a circuit-riding preacher who supports a wife at home."

Felicity's heart dropped to her stomach to land hard on the dinner she wished she hadn't eaten. Had she only thought she'd given up hope on Ben?

Well, his words pounded the nail into that coffin.

CHAPTER 3

With darkness shrouding Ft. Laramie, Ben, hands clasped behind his back, shoulders hunched, boots thudding like a blacksmith's hammers, trod the wooden boardwalk through the small town. He strode for over an hour, but God remained silent about his predicament.

He passed the general store for the fourth time. Light from a kerosene lantern in the window streamed on Felicity's sign. *Wanted Groom. All expenses paid.* The words flamed a trail into his heart.

Had he trudged here on purpose? Before he left his cold dinner lying on the table at Sal's boardinghouse, he'd jammed his big foot in his mouth about that sign. He'd laughed. But that had been before Felicity acknowledged *she'd* placed the sign in the window.

She'd dropped hints for the past two months that she liked him, but he'd turned a blind eye, and focused his thoughts on obeying God's will for his life. Now everything had changed.

Heart stampeding inside his chest, he closed his eyes. *God, do You want me to marry Felicity?*

The word *marry* felt foreign in his thoughts and rattled around in his mind.

Once on the trail, would the delightful lady change her mind and travel to the gold rush rather than to the free farmland? He had to pay off those medical bills, and a gold rush camp had great need of a preacher.

God, if You want me to wed

Felicity, You need to give me solid direction.

Felicity was a beautiful lady. She possessed a sunny disposition. Appeared to be a hard worker. And he enjoyed being in her presence. Had been a hard row to hoe to turn her down.

But he knew nothing about farming. He knew horses and the ins and outs of the part-time sheriff's job he'd taken while attending the University of Missouri. He knew how to preach. He'd had to quit seminary before he received his degree because Mother needed him when her health deteriorated due to the cancer growing inside her chest. But God's calling didn't depend on a degree. Or a wife.

Ben leaned closer to the store window. Quite a hubbub inside the general store. Lanterns glowed on the counters. Moving shadows showed men milling about inside. Golden hair gleamed behind the front counter. A trick of light fell on Felicity's angelic face.

Throat suddenly dry, he gulped. She wasn't waiting until morning. She was at this moment interviewing men to wed! She meant to follow through with her hare-brained scheme.

He pressed his nose to the glass window. Ft. Laramie was one tough frontier stopping-off place filled with desperadoes as well as good men. Perhaps one of those men inside was the thief who stole everything he owned. Another might be a murderer. Maybe the man she chose would be a wife-beater or a wife-deserter? What kind of man would he be to let Felicity fall victim to her own scheme? He was a God-fearing man in need of transportation to the west. He would treat Felicity with kindness. He would protect her. If she didn't know the Lord, he would lead her into God's flock.

Felicity needed him. Any one of

those other men could take advantage of such a naïve girl. He would not. He shook his head. Was his change of heart a sign that God wanted him to love and honor that silly girl?

A number of men poured out of the store. Ben slid into the shadows as Felicity and Jed walked from the store and down the sidewalk. Must be she'd finished her interviews.

With Felicity's hand tucked into Jed's arm, the couple headed toward Sal's. Bedtime then. Would Felicity sleep easy tonight with her choice already made?

Ben slipped inside the general store and passed groups of men hunched together and making bets on which of them beautiful, rich Felicity would choose as her husband.

"Okay, fellas, time to head out. Store's closing for the night. Miss Felicity will be back early tomorrow." The owner, Trevor McVey, herded the remaining men toward the door.

So, the compelling lady had not yet chosen a groom. A shadow lifted from Ben's heart.

He hustled to the counter. Pulling one of the child's chalkboards in front of him on the counter, he grasped a stub of chalk and wrote: *I owe you one ten-dollar gold piece. Ben Bonneville.*

God, if this is what You planned for me, let Felicity choose me as her husband. If not, show me another way to travel to the California gold fields. Felicity doesn't look like a farmer's wife to me. But she doesn't belong at the gold fields either. The beautiful lady should live back east ordering about a mansion of servants.

You know I've been praying about her for two months now. I think she should go back to Missouri. Oregon Territory's too rough for a lady like her.

Nevertheless, if Felicity continued on west, he had a mind to be the one driving her wagon. Much as he'd like to charge over to Sal's boardinghouse, beat on Felicity's door, and persuade her to be his wife, he would leave her decision in God's hands.

He strode toward the stable. His landlady, Sal, hadn't wasted any time. She'd kicked him out.

Since he'd already paid for Salvation's stall, he'd spend the night in the empty space.

Probably Felicity would erase his name from the chalkboard. He had little to offer her.

CHAPTER 4

Felicity ambled toward the general store. The gorgeous September morning, so clear the mountains rose purple in the distance, did little to lighten her heart. Today she must choose a husband. She'd tossed on her bed all night and had even hit the top of her head on the iron headboard. Her covers had knotted, and the room stifled her, though she'd thrown both windows wide open.

She'd splashed tepid water onto her face and brushed and arranged her waist-long hair into its usual braid.

She'd arrived downstairs before any of the other boarders and eaten a cold biscuit before her stomach rebelled.

Though Ben had been robbed, he'd not appeared at the store last night. Surely after he lost all his worldly goods, God would have spoken to him about signing up to become her husband. Tomorrow she must wed, and today she had to interview the ten men she'd selected. What was wrong with Ben? His chiseled features and broad shoulders had ensnared her heart. His athletic build could work any farm. Was she the problem? Did he not find her attractive?

The bell above the door tinkled, and she strolled into the store. The place looked a shambles. Men last night had moved the kegs they set on into small circles to discuss their chances. Her basket of gold pieces, and the chalkboards still cluttered the counter. Felicity heaved a deep sigh. Well, she would do what she must. Again, Ben lost his chance. She shrugged. Why would she want to wed a man who missed so many opportunities? She closed her eyes and his picture flashed before. Because the man stirred her heart into frenzy each time he came near.

She moved over to the counter and picked up the chalkboard with the ten names written on it.

Jedidiah lumbered up from the rear of the store. "Are you ready for this, Missy?"

"Yes. One of these men I interview, I shall have to marry."

Behind her, the bell above the door clanged. She turned.

Ben strode in. Two days' growth of dark beard shadowed his strong jaws. His eyes looked blood-shot, and his dark hair stood on end as if he too had spent a sleepless night. His boots clumped across the wooden floor, and he touched a light finger on her hand that held the chalkboard.

"You can add my name to that list."

Her heart leaped like a rabbit to fresh flowers. "Oh? Do you want transportation to Oregon?" She made her voice sound cool and unconcerned, but her stomach fluttered, and her hands turned icy. "I thought you planned to join the California Gold Rush."

"I do." His Adam's apple made an obvious trip up and down his tanned throat. "But I'd like to strike a bargain with you. If you choose me as your husband, after we're married and if you still have your heart set on getting to Oregon Territory, I'll see that you get there. But God might have other plans for us. I'd like you to be open to them."

Ben flashed his heart-stopping grin. "You won't be sorry if you choose me as your husband."

Her cheeks burned. "I promised to interview these other ten men. Shall I interview you as well?"

"That seems fair." He glanced around the store, empty except for Jedidiah standing next to her. "Why not start now? None of the others know you as well as I do. And they're not here." He glanced down at his rumpled clothes and red tinged his cheeks.

Had he slept in them?

"Sorry I look so ill groomed, but I've got nothing to change into, and Sal kicked me out of my room last night."

Her pulse raced. Drat! She *was* his last resort. Certainly not the way she'd hoped to find a husband. Perhaps she'd do better if she chose a man who wanted *her* as much as he wanted his expenses paid to gold rush Territory?

"Then, where did you sleep?"

"Slept in the stable. Still have my job there for two more days." He smiled.

He did have a warm, charming smile. Still had all his teeth, and they looked white and straight.

"Okay." She pulled a clean slate over and poised the chalk. "What are your qualifications?"

Again, his Adam's apple traveled his tan, muscular throat. "My qualifications?"

"Why yes. I'll weigh your qualifications against the other ten men and decide which of you would be best suited for a husband."

A bead of sweat formed at his hairline. He did have wonderful, wavy, dark hair.

"Qualifications?" He dragged a hand through that thick, dark hair, leaving a racetrack from front to back. "Well, as your husband…" he hesitated "…un…"

"You've never been married?"

"Of course not."

"What type of work do you do?"

"Preach…sheriff…clerked in stores…"

"Ever saw down trees?"

"Yeah, one or two."

"Build houses or barns?"

"Helped neighbors."

"Plow fields?"

"No."

"Plant fields?"

"No." Another trickle of sweat joined the first one.

The bell above the door clanged, and two muscular men strode in. Seeing them at the counter, they clomped over. "We're here for the interview."

Felicity smiled. "Would you mind waiting a few minutes? This interview shouldn't take long."

The men strode over to an overturned barrel. One sat. The other leaned against the wall. Both men had shaved, worn new shirts, and shined their boots. They stared at her, interest stamped on their faces.

Felicity turned back to Ben. "Now, Ben, is it?"

He nodded.

"You know how to drive a prairie wagon with horses?"

"Yes, I know horses."

"And driving a loaded prairie wagon?"

"Well, no. But I've driven a stagecoach. Can't be too different."

"You have a lot of nos checked against you. What do you do well?"

Ben tugged a hand through his hair again and frowned. "I learn fast."

The doorbell tinkled again. Three burly men clomped in.

"Have you given up your hope to take the Oregon Trail turn-off to California? Or do you still plan to prospect for gold?"

Ben's sea blue gaze turned stormy and dropped to the floor. "I'll cross that bridge when I come to it." He pinched the bridge of his nose and then glanced at her. His broad shoulders drooped. "I'm not a charity case. I'll give you more than my passage in work. By the time we hit the fork in the trail, *if* you still want to get that free land in Oregon, we'll go for it together."

"But in the meantime, you'll try to sway me into heading to California and forgetting about Oregon?"

"I can't lie to you, ma'am. That's exactly what I plan to do."

"And if I still want that land in Oregon, you'll go with me and sign up as my husband?"

His teeth ground. "If that's what you and the Lord want, then I'll take you on to Oregon Territory." Both his hands fisted on the counter, and his jaw clenched until the muscle bulged.

The bell clanged, and a rush of tall, strong men entered the store.

She smiled her sweetest smile. "I'll let you know."

His handsome face tight, his back like a ramrod, Ben turned to leave.

CHAPTER 5

"Where's Ben Bonneville?" A loud voice called.

Ben dropped the pitchfork full of hay and strode from Salvation's empty stall. "Right here. Who wants me?"

"Miss Daniels over at Sal's boardinghouse says to come immediately. The Fort Commander's ready to perform the wedding."

Ben's heart thundered. Salvation was gone, but the other horses hadn't been fed and needed fresh water. Still, how often did a man have a wedding? And the beautiful princess chose him.

Why hadn't she notified him? If she had, his straw bed last night would have been a featherbed, rather than a torture rack. "Be right there."

He stumbled over to the water trough and splashed water over his head and hands. No mirror, so he finger-combed his hair. He ran a hand over the rough bristles on his face. Fine-looking groom he made. His rumpled clothes smelled. He probably looked as if he'd been on a week-long binge. No help for it. Felicity chose him.

He dunked one boot into the water trough to get rid of the muck, and then the other. He'd give the horses clean water after he was a married man. He shivered. Blasted cold in the stable this morning.

Well, he'd done all he could to get ready.

He opened the stable door.

Outside everything glistened white. Snow layered the boardwalk, the roofs, the buildings, the street, the trees. Washed white. Yesterday had been hot. Today an unseasonable snow blanketed everything as far as he could see. Who knew weather in Wyoming was so changeable? Like the woman he was about to marry.

Yesterday, he'd been certain he'd lost the lottery. So he'd put in another sleepless night praying Felicity would find a man who would treat her well. A man who would protect her. A man who would love her. He'd not told her so in the interview, but if he had to kick the man she chose from kingdom come, nothing would keep him from making sure that man she married treated her well.

He stomped through ankle-deep, fresh, sparkling snow toward Sal's. He should be wearing a fine tailored suit, have a fresh haircut and shave, and be rested and ready to take on Felicity as his bride.

Nevertheless, his heart sang a psalm

of thanksgiving. The beautiful, spunky lady with the golden hair would be *his* wife! Fresh cold air stung his cheeks as he marched through the heavy snow. Had been the hardest task of his life to avoid her and refuse her offers of courtship. He'd thought the Lord wanted him to pan gold alone. But having a woman to bring gold nuggets home to was so like God. God always gave more than he expected.

Snow tumbled from the roof overhanging the boardwalk onto the back of his neck. He needed his jacket, but the thief swiped that too. Yet he thanked the thief. How else would he have known God wanted him to wed Felicity?

The wind crawled through his summer shirt. He shivered. Only a few more blocks to Sal's. Inside would be warm. Big, round flakes fell on his face. Slow at first, then heavier and thicker. Beautiful, but cold. He broke into a run, his boots sliding on the snowy boardwalk.

~

Felicity waited at the top of the wooden staircase at Sal's. The Commanding Officer of Ft. Laramie waited, Bible in hand, in front of a roaring fire in the good-sized living room. Men who had hoped to be chosen as her husband filled every available chair and stood in groups at the back. Perhaps they hoped Ben would not show?

Felicity shifted her weight. Her new white kid lace-up boots pinched. She smoothed her white dress, the only one available in Ft. Laramie, though the garment was only a white print with tiny white flowers. She'd ironed the flowing gown hastily. Still the garment fit well and looked smart.

But where was her groom? Had he left Ft. Laramie last night when he thought he'd not be chosen? Where could he have gone with his money and horse stolen? She'd remember today's date, September 2, 1850. This would be her wedding date, and she would celebrate this day until she went to be with the Lord. Oh, how she prayed she'd made the right choice. Every one of the other men had more to offer. But only Ben caused her pulse to race and her heart to warm. Not to mention the butterflies that flew in her tummy each time she gazed into his azure-blue eyes.

She turned to look out the tall window behind her. Where was Ben? No Ben, but the Lord sent the glorious snowfall as a promise of a new life with a new husband, and a new, permanent home of her own.

Was Ben perverse enough to make her wait as she had made him wait? The moment he entered the General Store last night, she'd known she would choose him. Why hadn't she told him then?

She tapped her foot. She'd give him five more minutes, then she'd—

The front door burst open, blowing in cold wind and snow. Ben stepped inside, put his shoulder to the door and forced the rough plank closed behind him. He blinked, gazed around the room, and then his sapphire eyes shot up to meet hers.

Cold blasted his handsome face red, he wore no jacket, and snowflakes melted into wet spots on his summer-weight shirt, outlining the athletic frame beneath. He pulled off his big hat. The dark hair below glistened as if he'd just had a shampoo and bath. His summer blue eyes held a light she'd never seen. Even the dark curtain of whiskers shadowing his face didn't detract from the grin that spread across his face. Did his bristles hide dimples? Oh, she had a lot to learn about this breath-taking man.

"Leave your guns at the door." The CO's booming voice probably carried all the way to the stable for the horses to hear.

Ben's hands moved so fast, his guns hung on the peg by the door before Felicity had even begun to admire Ben's lean hips and muscular legs.

"Thank you, Father God," she breathed. Didn't hurt that her groom was the best-looking man in the room. Didn't matter he'd never plowed or planted. He could learn.

His intense eyes blazed a trail up the stairs to her.

She started her slow descent to him.

A muted "Umm" rose from the men gathered in the lobby below. The men stood.

She had eyes only for Ben.

As her best man, Jed stroked his silver mustache and cleared his throat.

She met Ben in front of the CO. The fire's warmth reached out to meet them.

"Please face each other."

They already were.

The preacher placed their hands together. "Please hold hands."

His hands felt icy, but his lips smiled.

"Dearly beloved, we gather together to see this man and this woman united in holy matrimony…."

He'd never looked at her that way before. *Oh, thank you, God. This is the man you've chosen for me.*

"…I now pronounce you man and wife. You may kiss the bride." The CO moved away from the fire as if the blaze had been warming his backside too much.

She'd never kissed except that one time when she was ten and stepped under the mistletoe by mistake, and the neighbor's boy had run over and smacked his lips on hers. Ugh. She'd wiped that kiss off in a hurry.

Ben planted his arms around her as if he would never let her go and moved his lips ever so slowly down to hers.

She entwined her arms around his

neck and kissed him back until her body tingled.

Men around the room expelled a breath.

His cold lips warmed against hers and were soft and tender, full of promise. He lifted his head far too soon. When she opened her eyes, a deep flush darkened his face.

Her pulse whistled through her veins like a windy night full of snow. This was no mistletoe kiss. This was a forever kiss.

The men were supposed to clap, but a deep silence filled the room.

She was Mrs. Ben Bonneville, and she would own land in Oregon and have a permanent home for the first time in her life. And she'd be bound to the vibrant man standing beside her for as long as they both lived. She inhaled a shaky breath. What would marriage be like for them? She really did not know what kind of man Ben actually was.

A strong masculine odor filled her nose. He needed a bath. But she liked his scent.

The tall clock in the nearby nook chimed ten.

Outside huge flakes of snow fell silently against the window, whirling away into whiteness.

One by one the unchosen men filed out of the living room until only the four of them remained. She, Ben, Jed, and the CO.

"Um, I've got some things to attend to. If you need anything else, Ma'am, just send for me." The CO clasped his Bible in one hand and shook Ben's with the other. "Congratulations, man, you've married a fine woman."

"Thank you, sir. That I have."

Jed shook Ben's hand. "You take care of this woman, or I'll shoot a hole in you big 'nough to drive a wagon through."

"Yes, sir. You have no worries on that score. I'll take care of this angel with my life."

Jed nodded, then backed out of the room, his stern eyes never leaving Ben's face.

Then she was alone with a man for the first time in her life. Not just any man, but with Ben. Her husband. What would they do now?

The way he gazed at her sent delighted shivers all over her body. Might she invite him to her room at Sal's?

Or should she tell him their marriage would be in name only?

CHAPTER 6

Felicity gazed at the man she'd chosen to wed. Handsome, personable, and now penniless, he owed everything to her. No farmer, but by the looks of him a man who could carry his own weight physically. Extremely attractive and with a last name Pa's enemy couldn't trace back to her.

And he needed a bath.

He sat next to her on the horsehair settee. Behind them the floor clock ticked loud in the silence.

The other residents at Sal's kept peeking through the doorway from the dining room and gazing down over the banister from upstairs. "The other boarders would like to use the sitting room, but they are polite enough to give us time alone." She unclasped her tightly gripped hands where they rested in her lap and gazed at her ringless fingers.

"Uh huh." His face heated until even his ears turned scarlet.

"Should we go upstairs to my room?"

He shook his head as if he'd awakened from a dream. "Maybe I could head on over to the Purple Sage Saloon and mosey into the back room where they keep tubs and run baths for two bits a soak."

She nodded. "That's a fine idea. You would probably return by lunch time, and we could meet at Sal's dining table." Was he as reluctant to be alone with her as she was to be alone with him? True she knew Ben slightly better than any of the other groom applicants, but he was almost a stranger.

He sat, hands splayed on his jean thighs, back straight, face scarlet, gazing into the fire.

When he didn't make a move to leave, she stood. "Well, I shall meet you at lunch then."

He rose and dipped his head. "I'm sorry to ask, but do you have two bits for the bath and shave?"

"Oh!"

"I'm sorry. I can take a cold bath in the stable. Forget I asked."

"But just look outside. It's snowing huge flakes. I'm nervous the snowfall won't allow us to get started along the trail tomorrow." She glanced around the sitting room. Where had she left her glass-beaded reticule? She could ask Sal for a tin bathtub and hot water, but then Ben would have to strip and bathe in her small room. That simply wouldn't work.

Oh yes, there her purse was, on the

mantle shelf where she'd deposited the small bag when she'd gone upstairs to make her entrance for her groom. "I have just what you need here." She took her purse, found the twenty-five cents and placed the coins in his hand.

"Thank you." He clinked the money in his big palm. "I'll pay back every cent I borrow." His jaw tightened. "I've never been in this position before, and I won't ever be in this position again." He turned on his heel and headed for the front door. "Snow won't stick. We'll be on the road tomorrow at dawn."

The door shut behind him with a decisive bang.

She pulled in deep breaths. Well, he was a proud man. She'd learned that much about him. That trait could be either good or bad. Weak-kneed, she plopped down on the settee.

Jed made enough noise to scare a deaf deer as he entered the sitting room from the dining room. "Well, honey, how's it feel to be a married lady?" He slid down to sit beside her, his familiar form as comforting as a mug of mulled cider on Christmas Day.

"Now that we're married, I don't know what to do with him. The situation feels so awkward. I don't know Ben at all."

"Don't you fret, honey. I wouldn't let you marry a man I didn't think measured up. From all I've heard about Ben, he'll stick with you until they cut ice in Death Valley. He's a good man."

"Thanks." She reached for Jed's hand.

"Most men are like a prickly hedge. They have their good points. My take on young Ben is that he's got a oversupply of good points. Where'd he go?"

"He went to the Purple Sage for a bath and a shave."

"You sent him *out* for a bath?" Jed shook his head until his silver mustache flew straight out.

"Yes." Felicity straightened her back. "I'm not ready to be alone with him."

Jed rubbed her hand. "Well, honey, that's yer business." He winked. "Ben's good around horses and drives the stage from time to time when Wells Fargo needs a substitute driver, so he won't have no trouble driving yer prairie schooner." He smiled, showing the gap where he'd lost a tooth on the bottom. "Make sure you get plenty of sleep tonight. We head out at dawn tomorrow." His gray eyes twinkled.

Heat burned her cheeks. "We'll be ready. Everything's packed in my wagon except the clothes I'll need tomorrow. I'm anxious to be on our way. The snow won't stop us, will it?"

"Naw. Soon as the sun comes out this afternoon, snow will melt. I've got all our supplies and water loaded. Jist need to hitch up those mules, climb aboard, and we'll be on our way."

"Good. We can't leave soon enough for me."

"Ben looked as jumpy as a bit-up bull in fly time when he left here. Is he getting cold feet?"

"No. He had to borrow money for his bath."

"Shoulda guessed that. A good man always wants to throw his own lasso. Well, honey, I'm out to check those wagons. You notice the man had no jacket?"

"Yes, I did. Perhaps I'll run over to the mercantile and make some purchases. What size do you estimate he wears?"

"Looks like an extra-large to me." Jed stood and patted her shoulder. "I'm on my way." He smiled. "You look like a jackrabbit about to bolt into tall grass. Being married's nothing to be a scared of. Easy as fallin' off a log. Jist relax. Everthing will work out jist fine."

~

Lunch had been awkward with everyone shooting glances at her and Ben and grinning like expectant sparrows watching a worm hole.

The glistening snow outside had turned to slush, and when the sun peeked through the clouds, melted into pools of dingy water. Much like Felicity felt. Worry lines crinkled her forehead. She had to get this understanding with Ben over with so she could breathe free and set her mind on tomorrow's trip.

As if Jed read her mind he said, "Felly, I aim to spend the afternoon checking out the wagons. Looks to me like you and Ben have some talkin' to do to iron out this marriage thing." He scooted back his chair and rose from the dining table. "I'll see you at the crack of dawn tomorrow out at the wagon train. We drew numbers ten and eleven in the procession. I'll drive behind you and Ben."

Ben nodded his dark head. His freshly cut hair waved back from his forehead. "Good spot. Not too much dust to choke on and far enough back in the line to be sure the trail ahead is drivable."

Felicity raised her brows. "Have you traveled by wagon train before?"

"Of course. I had my own wagon and mules before someone stole them. I did some scouting and hunting for Jason Seemont, the wagon master." He shrugged. "But Jason's train continued on a couple months ago. I stayed behind to earn enough money to carry on to California. Had everything I needed to join Caleb Grant's wagon train until robbers stole my stash." He fisted his hands. "Somebody sure wanted to go back east because I checked with Caleb and no one signed onto his train with my gear."

Felicity cringed inside. She knew

nothing of Ben Bonneville except he was tall, strong, and so good-looking he made her nerves tingle every time he came near. And he did seem to have some redeeming qualities that would help Jed and her travel on to secure that land in Oregon. But would he steal one of her wagons and take off to the California Gold Rush when they reached that fork in the trail, or would he keep his part of their strange bargain?

"I hear Caleb Grant runs a tight train. He's a good wagon master, and he's been over the Oregon Trail several times. We're in good hands." Ben seemed more comfortable talking with Jed than with her. Perhaps he hadn't been around women much.

Jed nodded and turned to leave. "Looks like Felly's in good hands, too." His worn boots clicked on the wooden floor until he shut the boarding house door behind him.

Felicity sighed. She'd hoped the

others would leave the table as well, but they roosted in their chairs like brooding hens and appeared as if they wanted to stay and watch the newlyweds. "Shall we go up to my room?"

Ben jumped up from his chair as if a scorpion had crawled down his neck. "I'm ready if you are." He helped her shove back her chair and offered his hand.

As they left the dining room and strode up the staircase to the rooms for the boarders, he held her hand. They strolled the long hall to her room at the end, his boots and hers tapping on the bare wooden floor.

Once inside the small room, Felicity folded her full skirts and perched on the edge of the double bed. She nodded toward the straight-backed chair. "Please sit down."

Ben turned the chair and straddled the reed seat, his brilliant robin's-egg blue eyes sizzled across the small space and fastened on her.

How to start? She'd thought downstairs was awkward! She couldn't meet that expectant gaze. Instead she glanced at the familiar rose wallpaper, the dresser with the washbasin, the cheval mirror, and down to the patchwork quilt on which she sat.

"You wanted to talk before—"

"Yes! Yes." She grabbed a hand full of her white gown and worried the soft material. "There's one small matter we need to clear up."

"And that is?"

He had a beautiful smile. Straight, white teeth. Slight impressions like dimples in his lean cheeks.

"Um, yes. This is rather delicate to put into words."

"Go ahead. I'm your husband. You can tell me anything. Whatever you need, I'll take care of it."

"I'm so happy to hear you say that. I do have rather an urgent need, and you are the only one who can ..." She hesitated. " … take care of it."

"Whatever you want. I'm your husband, and I'll provide it." His face beamed.

He really seemed to like her. How different his attitude had been when she'd tried to entice him into courting her. He scarcely seemed the same person. His vibrant presence overwhelmed the room. Seeing this charming, attentive side of him jolted her pulse to race so fast he must see it beat in her throat. She raised her hand to hide her throat. Was her heart hung in her throat because she was alone in a bedroom with a man for the first time? She wet her dry lips.

He arose and moved toward her, his hands out, his eyes wide, his mouth smiling.

"No, please sit. Hear me out."

He backtracked, dropped his hands, and straddled the reed-seated chair.

Would he grow angry? Would he hit her? The muscles she wanted for felling trees and planting crops bulged beneath the sleeves of his folded-back shirt sleeve. Would he use that strength to end their marriage before it even started? She'd heard stories in the evenings on the wagon train. And seen bruises.

No help for her predicament. She'd made her bed, now she had to sleep in it. "There's just one thing I need to tell you?"

A shadow crossed his face.

Was he a violent man? Jed was over at the wagon train, too far to help. He wouldn't look in on her until breakfast. Had she been too strong-willed and mule-stubborn? Had she made a terrible mistake?

His strong hands gripped the back of the chair with white knuckles.

"I don't know how to put this." Her voice trembled.

"Look, if you need a day to get acquainted, I can wait." His voice rasped as if the mellow baritone came from a tight throat.

"No. No. That's not it."

His taut face relaxed into another beautiful grin. "What's the problem then?"

"I should have told you before we said our vows."

His face darkened. "Are you expecting a baby?"

"No. No. Nothing like that. Far from it."

A frown formed between his dark brows. He leaned so far forward she hoped the chair wouldn't tip over. "Then what's the problem? Did you get robbed too?"

"No. Please, just relax. You're making this difficult."

He settled into the seat. His face hardened. His hands fisted around the chair back. "O.K., I'm relaxed. Tell me what's eating you."

He didn't look relaxed. Every muscle in his body stood on alert. Oh, she was handling this all wrong. She gazed down at the wad she'd made of the lap of her gown. His magnetic presence in her small room distracted her. She must pull herself together.

CHAPTER 7

Ben rubbed the back of his neck. His head pounded. The delicate, lovely young lady, by some miracle of God, his wife, sat in her virginal, white dress on the bed. He was alone with his wife. His wife! And he didn't dare touch even a shining strand of her glorious blonde hair until she got off her chest what bothered her.

He clenched his teeth. He would wait until she confessed whatever dark sin separated them before he took her in his arms, caressed her silky hair, and kissed her beguiling lips. But nothing she said would keep them apart. They had an entire lazy afternoon to themselves for their honeymoon before they drove out in that wagon train at dawn tomorrow.

Last night after he'd allowed his heart to feel, he'd known with every fiber of his being that he wanted Felicity as his wife. What warmed his heart must be love. And that deep ache that made him want the best for her, even if she didn't choose him had to be love. Certain last night, and even surer this morning that he wouldn't be chosen, shards like glass shredded his heart thinking of Felicity choosing first one and then another of the men he knew by sight and hearsay. All good men. She did know character when she saw it. Not a one of the potential grooms a murderer, thief, lazy, or mean. Each man had more to offer then he.

But she'd chosen him.

His heart thundered. Despite the

chill in the room, blood ran through his veins so hot and fast he perspired. His head swam. But he must be patient. Whatever bothered her appeared difficult for her to put into words. Was she fearful? "I will never hurt you."

"I thought not."

"I will always be faithful."

"I'm certain you will."

"As I get back on my feet, I'll provide for you, and I'll protect you."

"Thank you."

He jackknifed off the chair and knelt at her feet. "I realized last night that I love—"

"Stop!" She rose and turned her back to him. "I can't …"

He sprang to his feet, went to her, and touched her arm. "Go on."

She spun to face him. "My father insisted I marry. I need a driver for one of my wagons. I need a husband to gain the land I want."

"Yes, I understand all that." He cupped his hands around her upper arms. His hands tingled with her warmth.

She gazed up at him with wide, beautiful, hazel eyes. Frightened eyes. His heart hammered. She feared him! "Tell me."

"I prefer this marriage to be in name only. For the purposes I mentioned."

His arms dropped to his sides. Time ended. His world tilted.

"You need me, and I need you. We shall help each other. And that ... is ... all."

The silent room closed in like water drowning him. She didn't want him.

"Do I have your word?"

He shook his head but the whirling inside wouldn't stop. He was married for life. But not married? What limbo was this?

"Do I have your word?"

CHAPTER 8

Felicity walked beside the moving wagon. As a wife, for propriety's sake, she trudged by her husband's team and took turns with him at driving the mules. All day they'd plodded across a plain, so hiking hadn't been difficult.

She pulled in a deep breath of fall-scented air, mule odor, and axle grease. So wonderful being on the move again. The unseasonable snow had melted, and the day stayed pleasant with the thudding of hooves and the creaking of wheels and the wind whispering against the white canopy top of their prairie schooner.

The nine wagons ahead barely stirred up dust and strung out like a wavering ribbon in front of them. In the wagon behind, Jed's silver head and mustache bobbed as the older man nodded on the driver's seat, the reins loose in his hands.

A family walked beside the wagon in front. Their milk cow, tied to the rear of the wagon, ambled obediently in the shade of the wagon, tail switching back and forth. Pots and pans hanging from hooks along both sides of the canvas clanged a cheerful tune. Two little girls in gingham dresses looked enough alike to be twins, their long braids bouncing against their small backs as they walked. The mother, looking as if she were again in the family way, strolled at their sides.

Ben slapped the reins against obstinate black backs as her mules pulled to the side to nibble fresh, green grass. He wrestled them away from their grazing.

God was in charge, and the world looked fresh and clean with snow dripping from the branches of the pine trees they passed. She was finally on her way to gain that free land in Oregon.

But try as she would to rid herself of them, restless thoughts swirled inside her head. She retied the ribbons of her sunbonnet and peeked around the blue material at the man driving her team. Ben had appeared tireless and cheerful all day. The irresistible man started a conversation with her each time she glanced up at him. When they changed places, he walking and she driving, he handed her up into the wagon and down from the wagon in a most courteous manner. No one could have asked for a more desirable companion. Even easy-going Jed seemed cranky in comparison. And Ben took great care of the mules. He held the reins with a gentle hand and hopped down and led the eight ornery beasts when the column of covered wagons traveled up a long hill.

Mules weren't the only recalcitrant creatures she traveled with. Yesterday she'd glimpsed Ben's obstinate side. Mule-headed that's what he was. Stubborn to a fault. After a stunned silence when she'd delivered her news, his face had turned to stone. She'd insisted he promise her.

But he hadn't. With bulging jaw and narrowed eyes, he finally said, "I promise to court you until you love me as much as I love you. Until you do, I promise not to touch you."

A thrill flashed through her veins even now. How magnificent he'd looked. His blue eyes steeled to grey with purpose, his expression determined, his head thrown back as if nothing could stop him. Her heart had answered. But she'd stood toe to toe to him and neither had backed down.

Ben could be so easy to love. But

would he insist on splitting from the wagon train at Fort Hall and heading south to the California gold fields? He needed that quick money, and she needed that Oregon land for her permanent home. So far, she'd not been able to persuade him. And she refused to go to California. Were his needs greater than hers? No. She'd ached for a home of her own since Mother died when she was born, and Dad had dragged her around the country on his quest against outlaws.

So why, when Ben left her room with the excuse that he needed to work in the stable and earn a few last dollars, had she felt so alone? And yet, how relieved not to have him inside her bedroom.

She spent her wedding day ironing the warm clothes she bought him. And hoping no one noticed her new husband slept in the stable.

Felicity shook off her thoughts. Today was a new day. She glanced at the cloudless sky and smiled. The ex-sheriff with a grudge against Daddy that he'd exposed in a letter to the editor of the *Independence Times* would never find her as Mrs. Ben Bonneville. She'd escaped his clutches. And the revenge of whomever else tailed her father west. She had no idea who else or how many more. But they no longer worried her.

Still, if anyone should track her and uncover her past, Ben appeared more than able to protect her. What joy to have that burden lifted off her shoulders. Dear Jed would have risked his life for her, but her old friend was no match for men intent on vengeance.

With the sun dipping low in the west, she gave a little skip. God loved her, and life was good. With Ben acting more like a brother than a husband, she could endure the rest of this long journey.

If only she could rid herself of the nagging guilt. She should have told

Ben before they wed that she had no intention of consummating their marriage. But somewhere deep inside her heart, she'd known he wouldn't have married her if she'd revealed her entire plan. So, she'd kept silent. He must not discover her deathly fear of childbirth.

She pulled off her sunbonnet and let the breeze stir her hair. Mama died when she was born, leaving her terrified to become with child. She'd planned never to wed. Only her desperation drove her to Ben. But guilt grew stronger each day as he attempted to win her love.

He was so captivating.

"Wagons circle. Wagons circle." Caleb Grant, the wagon train master, called as he trotted by on his sorrel mare.

The welcome word relayed down the long line of wagons. She'd soon have a fire going and prepare the evening meal. Perhaps they would sing hymns around the campfire as they had when Daddy traveled with them. Perhaps they would dance.

She shivered. How would she feel dancing with Ben? Was he graceful and quick-footed or awkward? Would he like dancing with her as the square dance master called the steps to *Nobody's Darlin' But Mine*?

Did he dance the Schottische or the waltz? How she loved to dance after a long day's trek. Her worn feet took on new life when she unlaced her walking boots and shoved her feet into her dancing slippers. And tonight, after two months stuck in Ft. Laramie, her feet begged to dance.

Had Ben danced with many women? He was so attractive he was certain to have enjoyed many girls' attention. She caught her breath. Yet he'd said he loved her. How had that happened?

Her gaze wandered to where he was unhitching the mules, giving them a good rubdown, and leading them to a meadow with a stream where he would hobble them, then carry them some grain. Watching him was pure pleasure. Funny she'd never thought other men looked so easy on the eyes while being efficient in their work. He glanced at her now and again and offered a warm smile and a wave of his masculine hand. The red-checked shirt she'd bought him fit his broad shoulders as if the flannel had been tailored to his size.

Each time he smiled, her stomach fluttered, and she discovered a return smile on her face.

Oh, she must stop staring and get the beans she'd half-cooked in the kettle over the fire and the coffee in the pot. Plus, she had to soak tomorrow night's ration of beans.

The man was so helpful. Immediately after he'd pulled the mules to a halt and set the hand brake, he'd raced to the river and carried back two pails of water for her to use.

She, Jed, and Ben made a warm family group as they gathered around the campfire she'd built, and ate from their tin plates, and drank hot coffee from their tin cups.

Ben brought in more kindling and fed the fire while he and Jed talked with deep, resonant voices about men things.

She rested on a blanket, bracing her back against a fallen log, and enjoyed gazing overhead as stars peeked out one by one, shifting the black sky into a twinkling blanket of beauty.

In the center of their circle of wagons, the fiddlers tuned their instruments. Tonight they played hymns rather than square dances. She discovered Ben sang with a musical baritone and knew all the hymns she knew plus some she did not. They sat side by side on a log in a huge circle with the other families. Jed sprawled on the grass next to her.

Would Ben hold her hand? She laid her fingers near enough to touch his knee, and he took her hand in his warm, masculine fingers. How pleasant to have a big man hold her hand as if he treasured it. Tonight, she didn't even miss Papa.

Ben was proving to be a wonderful man. She'd made the right choice.

Maybe Papa had been wrong when he preached *Dreams never amount to much. They just get your hopes high until someone comes along and stomps them into the ground. Get you some land and work out your own dream. Quit stargazing and come down to earth.*

Being here with Ben was no longer a dream. This was lovely reality. Together, they'd file for that free land, move onto the lush acreage, and make the opulent land their own.

Only one thing could shatter her dream.

An obstinate husband.

CHAPTER 9

Ben grunted. They'd been on the trail six weeks now, and, as far as he could tell, his courting Felicity hadn't made any headway.

He wiped perspiration from his forehead from straining his shoulder against the slippery wheel. He'd worked a good half-hour helping the mules get the wagon across the muddy creek bed. He arched his back. Not easy work. He bent to the task.

He showed her every way she let him that he loved her. But she didn't appear convinced.

The wagon rocked.

"I should climb down and walk. You don't need my extra weight in the wagon." Felicity's anxious face, shaded by her blue sunbonnet, gazed down at him.

He loved her beautiful hazel eyes. Never seen any others that came near to that clear, honest color. "No. You'll get wet and muddy. You don't weigh enough to make a difference in lightening the wagon. Stay put and don't fall if the wagon tilts."

He grunted and strained until the sucking mud let the wheel loose and the wagon jerked and slanted on across the wide stream. He pushed against the rear end until Felicity's wagon moved up the slippery riverbank, then turned back to help Jed's wagon cross the mud that clutched like giant hands.

He'd be exhausted by nightfall. That was good. Took every ounce of strength he had to keep his hands off his bride. When she climbed into the wagon to turn in for the night, her hair spilled down her back in a magnificent waterfall of blonde curls. He had the right to caress those curls, but she didn't love him yet. So, he couldn't even touch one wisp. He pulled in a deep breath. Maybe she never would.

Each night he tossed and turned on his bed of pine needles beneath the wagon thinking of her just above, just out of reach. His own wife, and he couldn't even touch her hair. Drove him wild. Kept him awake until exhaustion took over. Then she filled his dreams.

She was so beautiful with her delicate face, large hazel eyes, pert little nose, and luscious lips. His fingers ached to stroke her silky skin. He wanted to draw close to her as only a husband and wife could. Each day she seemed to look forward more to his presence. The nights around the campfire tested him to the utmost. Dancing with her so light on her feet, and his arm around her tiny waist, singing hymns, harmonizing with her lilting soprano, or just sitting around the crackling fire with friends chewing the fat, made no difference. He wanted his wife. Would she never accept him? Time blundered to a halt, waiting for her.

No matter how hard the trail, she never complained, though she had to be worn out at the end of each day's long haul. As the country grew rougher, she walked most of the day. She didn't have the expertise to drive the wagon over the mountains and down into the valleys. Keeping the mules in line and on the trail and the wagon from dropping off a mountain was about more than he could manage. Fortunately, Jed had driven mules all his life. Ben valued any advice the old man gave.

Ben called, "Get up there, Jenny. Get up there, Jake. You mules get back on the road." He worked the eight heavy reins, getting the mules back on the trail. He'd been afraid for Felicity that time the Indians made a surprise visit. But she'd stayed calm, even when the leader strode over to touch her hair. After that, when Indians rode into camp or beside the train, she whisked her hair into a knot and tied her sunbonnet on, hiding her hair.

His empty stomach rumbled. Felicity cooked some mighty fine beans, fried taters, and cornbread over the campfires. Tonight, she would cook the brace of quail he'd shot. Food fit for a king. He slammed his Stetson back on his head. Felicity outshone all the other pretty ladies on the train. He'd had to give warning to a couple fellas who eyed her like she was a Christmas Plum Pudding.

In all his twenty-four years, he'd never given a thought to taking a bride. Now every waking minute she monopolized his thinking. He hadn't even thought about preaching to the people accompanying them on the train. He was remiss. Sinful, not to be about the Lord's business. But Felicity jammed his thinking.

And that land in Oregon, you'd think that was the Promised Land the way she carried on about it. Would she choose to go with him to California? Two weeks ago, he'd been certain she would fall for him faster than chain lightning with a link snapped and be happy to follow him to the gold fields.

Now he was far from certain.

He wiped a muddy hand over his face. He *had* to pay off Ma's debts, half of which built-up due to the hired help she'd needed. The debt rode like a four-story building on his shoulders. He owed seventy-five dollars to various medical people. Take a farmer years to pay off that debt. More likely when the bill collector came, he'd lose that free land Felicity so wanted. He'd never farmed. Never wanted to. He could fell trees and build a credible log cabin. But putting his shoulder to a plow and knowing when to plant and when to harvest ... like a foreign language to him. He was a preacher. And he needed gold, not grain.

Wind whipped his Stetson off again. The Stetson she'd bought.

He wrapped the reins around the brake handle, jumped from the driver's seat, and took off running to catch the ten-gallon hat. The brim caught on a prickly pear cactus. He wiped his muddy hands on his filthy pants and used two fingers to disentangle the big hat from the cactus and set his possession back on his head. He couldn't control his life, but he could sure control his hat.

He gazed up as heavy clouds blanked out the sun. Lowering skies crackled with lightning.

Where had that storm come from so suddenly?

He raced back to the wagon train. The procession crawled in front like a twisting snake up a mountain. Big drops of rain stung his face. Sleet.

Felicity must have shimmied up to drive in his place to keep the wagon in line. "Felicity, I'll drive now. You climb back into the wagon and stay dry. Looks like a storm's kicking up."

The wagon slowed. Felicity's face showed relief. She called, "Whoa. Whoa there." The mules stopped, and she set the brake.

He leaped up to the driver's seat, gathered up the two hands full of reins, and watched her maneuver into the wagon under the canopy, her full skirts whipping in the wind. In the wagon ahead, that entire family of girls jumbled up in their wagon peeked over the tailgate. They didn't even stop their slow-moving oxen while the older son dived onto the driver's seat beside his father.

Closing the gap between their wagons, he shivered. Temperature had dropped at least twenty degrees in the last half hour. This promised to be a big storm. The afternoon grew darker than a blacksmith's apron.

Rain spit from the sky as if nature were mad enough to fight like an Indian on the warpath. The deluge wet him through to his skin in seconds. The brim of his hat hung low, flattened by splattering sleet. Fresh scented air whipped his wet shirt against his skin. The mules lowered their heads, laid back their long ears, and plodded on. If this downpour kept up, even the double canvas rubbed with linseed oil wouldn't keep the sleet out, and Felicity and all her goods would get drenched. He could do nothing but keep the ice-slicked reins clutched in his fists, hold the ornery mules on the trail, and hunch against the pounding sleet. He could barely make out the wagon moving ahead.

On this mountainside there was no place to pull aside and camp. Their train had no choice but to keep moving. And with these sleet-slicked roads, the way down would be treacherous.

CHAPTER 10

Felicity huddled beneath a quilt. How had it gotten so cold so suddenly? Would this sleet turn to snow? Darkness grew inside the wagon so she could barely make out the trunks and barrels. Had life been too easy? Dreams been so close as to seem to come true. Would the whole train die on this mountain? Had Papa been right about dreams?

Lightning creased the sky. Thunder immediately boomed. A tree snapped and fell not far away.

Above the hissing rain came another sound. Was that Ben's teeth chattering? She lifted the front canvas flap and peeked out. His whole body shivered. He would catch pneumonia. When the next flash lit the sky, she groped in the trunk and fished out the winter jacket she'd bought for him. Inching forward over the trunks, barrels, and boxes she picked her way over the packed goods to the front opening.

"Put this on," she shouted over the noisy torrent of sleet.

He turned his sky-blue gaze on her.

Those eyes etched a path directly to her heart.

He shook his head, sending streams of water flying in all directions. "I'm too wet. I'll ruin that good coat."

"Then crawl back here and dry off. The train's moving so slow you'll be on the driver's seat again in no time."

Actually, the train had stopped. The mules stood, heads lowered, ears almost touching the ice-crusted mud beneath their feet. A thin blanket of sleet coated the mud.

Ben wrapped the reins around the brake and climbed inside. The wagon tilted with his weight. He slithered over some barrels, leaned on the corner of one, the coat held out to keep the heavy material from getting wet. Rain dripped off his face and clothes into a puddle onto the floorboards. "I hate to get this fine sheep-skin coat wet."

"I won't abide you catching pneumonia. Take off that wet shirt." She handed him a towel.

His long fingers shook as he tried to unbutton his shirt.

She pushed his hands aside and unfastened the buttons.

He peeled off the wet flannel and handed the dripping shirt to her. She opened the back canvas drape, leaned her arms out, wrung the shirt over the mud, and then draped the shirt over a trunk. All the while trying not to watch how Ben's muscles flexed as he dried his torso. She handed him his dry shirt, and he slipped the green, checked flannel on. She buttoned his buttons. He shrugged into the coat.

Then he leaned over, cupped his cold hands around her face, and kissed her. His lips were cool but grew warm and tender. The lightning that flashed was inside her heart, not outside the prairie schooner.

Astonishing new feelings burst through her. His kiss promised, he had not lied. He loved her.

Too soon he moved away. "That's thanks for the coat!"

Was her imagination running amuck, or did his voice shake?

Almost as soon as the storm caught them unawares, the rain ended.

He crawled back out onto the driver's seat and slapped his dripping Stetson on his head.

She tried not to think of the hungry look in his eyes or the satisfied smile on his lips.

She opened the canvas flap in time

to see a perfect rainbow arch across the eastern sky. Such delicate colors. Her heart reflected the beautiful colors. And she so enjoyed his kiss. Her lips still felt warm. And sweet. She couldn't stop thinking of the wonder of being close to him.

The wagon jerked, slid and bumped. Soon the wagon bed tilted downward. They were descending.

She'd heard of mountaintop experiences with the Lord. She'd just had a mountaintop experience with Ben. Was she in love with the incredible man?

Her turn to drive, but she couldn't manhandle the wagon down the slippery slope. She had not the experience or the strength. With the sleet ended, she folded back the flap to catch more of the fresh, clean air.

Ben worked, feet braced against the floorboard, right hand grasping all eight reins, left hand alternating between the chain lock and the log drag, his face taut, his jaw set. At times, the wagon slid crosswise on the muddy trail and threatened to skid down the mountain. Ben kept control and worked the wagon back to the center of the road.

~

Their journey continued.

Felicity encountered new adventures day after day. Too soon they would reach the split in the trail at Fort Hall where a few of the wagons would turn south and lumber toward California. The rest of them would rumble north toward Oregon and the free land.

Ben kept his promise about swaying her to go to the gold rush with him. Each night before she retired to the wagon, and Ben crawled underneath to his cramped bed amid the spare parts, spokes, tongues, and axles slung under the wooden wagon bed, he talked about their traveling to California. He spoke of the rich nuggets waiting to be captured from the cold, rushing streams. He spoke of paying off his mother's debt. He grew passionate about preaching to the needy souls drawn to California by the lure of gold. He promised that after the debt was paid, he'd take her on to Oregon Territory to claim her six hundred forty acres of prime farmland.

She frowned. But, of course, by then all the free land would be claimed. They would be too late.

Through every day on the trail, Ben remained adamant they should travel on to gold rush country. The man continued to be mule stubborn.

What should she do? That single kiss made her soul sing until her silly heart flew right out of her breast and landed at his feet.

Could she follow Ben to an uncertain future? There was nothing in California for her. No land. No permanent home. No roots. Nothing but warring men killing themselves to dig up riches from the earth. Bawdy women. Lawlessness.

He promised to pay back every cent he owed her. He promised to take her to the Willamette Valley in Oregon if she was still bound to go. But he let her know he sure didn't want to go. He owed all that money. And God called him to preach.

How could she be selfish enough to insist Ben give up his dream to make her own dream come true? But Papa preached that land was the only reality. Everything else was stargazing. Papa made her promise to go on to Oregon and start a new life with Oregon land.

The night wind blew pungent odors of horses, unwashed men, wood smoke, and supper cooking over campfires to remind her.

Time had run out. She must choose between her heart and her head. Her dream and harsh reality.

CHAPTER 11

Ben shrugged his aching shoulders. Tomorrow the wagon train would split. If he drove her wagon south to California, would Felicity ride with him or would she choose to ride on to Oregon with Jed?

He'd promised if she didn't change her mind, he'd take her on to the Willamette Valley in Oregon and help her homestead that free land. His stomach roiled. Never wanted to farm. Didn't like the loneliness of living in the middle of nowhere, grinding a living from the dirt. God called him to preach. In order to deliver sermons, he had to be among people. Live in a mining camp or at least a town. He craved excitement. And he had to roll that debt off his back. Lots of men would write off that obligation and forget the responsibility. He couldn't.

But he had an obligation to Felicity, too.

He gazed down at her hiking along like a pioneer woman. Each day they drew nearer Oregon Territory, her face brightened until she glowed. Her contagious smile made his heart sing. Her happiness bubbled over.

When she was happy, so was he.

They'd barely completed the rough trek over the mountains before snowflakes drifted from the sky. The small boots Felicity wore trudged ankle deep in wet whiteness. Probably ice flows clogged the Snake River. At best, crossing that treacherous river at the ford near Ft. Hall was dangerous. He'd make certain Felicity crossed safely before he broke off from the train and headed southwest to California.

~

Felicity stared up at Ben sitting tall on the driver's seat with his Stetson low on his forehead, the four pairs of reins held in one hand. Which way would he choose to go?

Ben shifted on the wagon seat and glanced down. "That sun sure is welcome. I hear that much sunshine in November is unusual."

"I love feeling the warmth on my face."

"Yeah, feels good. But our train had too many delays along the trail, what with broken wagon wheels, and trading with the Indians to keep them from attacking."

"That was scary. But that bout with cholera that stopped us all for several days frightened me more." Thank God, neither she nor Ben nor even Jed had caught the fever.

"Right. We lost too many friends." Ben's words sounded clipped.

He'd lost several buddies to the awful diarrhea and had hovered over her until he made her uneasy.

"Snake River's looking angry this late in the season."

"Yes. Are we too late to cross?" If they had to camp this side and wait for spring all the good land would be claimed before she reached Oregon.

Ben gazed across the Snake River to the other side. "Still a long way to California." He glanced at her. "And to the Oregon Territory. Nope, we'll cross today. Got to. Might be our last chance."

Several chunks of ice rushed along the rapid current of the river. Felicity shivered. How would they pass through such a treacherous mountain of water? How could this raging current be the best ford? If only Moses were here to send them across on dry land.

"Scared?" Ben called down from his seat on her wagon.

"Yes. I can swim, but that looks icy and too swift for me."

"Looks bad, all right. But I'll see you and Jed safely across."

"Thanks!" But then what? He'd not given an inch on insisting they go to California, and she wasn't ready to ask about that again.

"Whoa, whoa there. Whoa, Jenny. Whoa, Jake." Ben halted the team of pig-headed mules. He climbed down to station himself beside Felicity as the wagon train halted parallel to the swiftly flowing river. "Probably take us all day, but we'll float the wagons across, and the teamsters will swim their livestock to the other side." His jutting chin turned toward her. "People have crossed at this point for several years." He touched her shoulder. "Some wagons get snagged and float down the river and are lost. Some hit boulders in the stream and overturn. I won't kid you, some people die here." He smiled. "We won't. I'll make sure both your wagons and you and Jed make it safe to the other side."

Tears pricked the back of her lids, and she blinked rapidly. "How can you promise such a thing?"

"I've been praying about this crossing and the split trail up ahead. God has work for us to do, so he won't let anything happen to us. He'll keep us safe."

Her heart skipped so many beats she felt faint. "I do hope you remember your promise. I've not changed my mind about going to Oregon."

He grunted. "Nor have I about hightailing it to California."

She lowered her head and pulled in some deep breaths. "What sort of work would God have for me in California?"

His eyebrows shot up, and his mouth tightened. Then he walked to each mule and spoke in an ear, running his hands over the places where they liked to be petted.

"Please tell me?"

He half-turned from the mule named Julie, one hand rubbing her ear. "You'd stay inside our tent and cook for me." He snatched off his Stetson and ran his fingers through his thick, dark hair. "You'd do our washing."

"At that icy stream you spoke of?"

He heaved a deep sigh. "Yes."

"Cook over a campfire?"

"Pretty much."

"And what shall we do with both wagon loads of household items?"

"We'd only prospect for a few months."

"What if you don't find any gold?"

"I will."

"What will I do when you are out preaching to the miners? I hear those mining towns are rough, and few women live there."

He frowned.

"What will you do when those bawdy, gold-digging women proposition you?"

Red flamed under the dark bristles on his cheeks. "You don't need to worry about any other women. I'm a married man. I won't look at a one of them."

She humphed. "And if those painted ladies pout their lips and tell you they need to be saved from their sinful life, you'll turn away?"

"No. I'll tell them how Jesus died for them, and no matter how much they've sinned, He loves them and will forgive them."

"And if these fallen women repent, what kind of work will they find to do in a mining camp?"

He shook his head. "You've really thought this through, haven't you?"

"Yes, I have, sir. And I'm certain a mining camp is no place for a God-fearing woman. Nor do I think that turbulent place suitable for a married man and his wife."

He shifted his stance, gazed down at his boots, scrunched his dark brows and avoided looking at her. "We'll have to talk later. It's our turn to cross. I have to drive the wagon down the bank and unhitch the mules." His sky-blue eyes clouded. "We need to hire some of those Indians to help float our wagons across." He turned and scrambled down the steep river bank to talk with a group of dripping Indians emerging from the river.

Jed moseyed up to plant his worn boots in the grass beside her. He stared at the wagons floating across the river and pulled on his silver mustache.

"Bless the man, Jed. Ben still thinks I'll go to that gold mining camp in California. Can you talk some sense into him?"

"I've been a talkin' a blue streak, Felly. The man's more stubborn than all our mules combined. He's so obstinate he wouldn't move camp for a prairie fire." He rubbed his silver-whiskered jaw. "Man's been reelin' round like a pup tryin' to find a spot to lie down. He wants to please you, but he's obligated to pay off that debt."

"Do you think we should go to California for a few months and then travel on to Oregon?"

"I wonder if we didn't make a big mistake when we chose Ben as your groom. Maybe should have chosen one of those other good men."

Perhaps Jed was right. Perhaps she'd made a huge mistake. But Ben had made a bargain.

And she wouldn't change her mind.

CHAPTER 12

Ben smothered the fear in his chest and plastered on an unconcerned expression.

"Climb on Jenny. She's the safest, most obedient mule in your team. Hang on to the reins, and Jenny will do the rest. She's a great swimmer."

He made a foothold for Felicity with his hands and boosted her onto Jenny's slender back. "I'll be praying the entire time you're in the river. The water will be icy, and you're bound to get numb, but Caleb Grant has a fire going on the other side. Head directly there." He held Jenny's bridle in one hand and rubbed her ear with the other. "After you cross, I'll get the rest of the mules across. After that, I'll join you at the fire." He laid a warm hand on her dress-covered calf, and then squeezed her booted foot. "The others have had no problems, and the river's fairly calm. This time of day is the best time to cross."

"But what about our wagons?"

"After you and Jed and the mules cross, I'll work with the Indians we hired to float our wagons across. The first nine wagons and teams made the crossing just fine. No reason we can't."

Except Felicity looked more delicate than any of the farmer's wives. And she was *his* wife. Almost his wife. He'd done his best, but he hadn't crossed that barrier yet.

"Stay calm, keep your reins loose and give Jenny her head. Leave the rest to me."

She smiled down at him, her creamy complexion pale, her cinnamon eyes begging him for his strength and protection. He'd ride with her if two on Jenny would help, but he'd be too much weight for Jennie in that swift-moving river. A cold knot squirmed all the way through his chest and wound around his heart. Crossing the Snake River was no place for the sweet woman he'd allowed himself to love. If anything happened to her ...

She gazed at him, trust in her hazel eyes. Her luscious lips formed into a delightful smile. But fear showed in the way her hands gripped the reins too hard and her knees strained around Jenny's barrel stomach.

"I'm praying for you, Felly." Jed straddled Joseph, their biggest mule, who thought he was a clown, but remained a steady, reliant beast. "I'll be side by side with you, Felly. No need to be frettin'."

Fear worked its way up to freeze

Ben's brain. He had to cross that icy river with the other three mules, then cross with both wagons, then cross again, five trips. But even prolonged frigid water wouldn't keep him from protecting Felicity.

If Felicity had the slightest trouble during her crossing, he had Jake reined and ready to ride. He couldn't stand the thought of Felicity's bright head going under water in that icy river. He hopped on Jake. "I'm crossing with you too. I'll ride on your upstream side."

Felicity nodded, gave him a wavering smile, glanced at Jed, and kicked her heels into Jenny's sides. "Get up, Jenny. We're going for a swim."

As Jenny's hooves touched the cold water, Ben's stomach clenched into knots. Felicity gasped as her legs submerged. Her long dress floated up over her knees, then grew wet and lumped down over her legs. A few steps more and water swirled around her waist.

He spurred Jake to the upside where the current blasted the hardest.

Jed moved to her other side. The mules lunged forward until they had to swim. He drove Jake next to Felicity, their mules almost touching. He must get his wife safely across.

Once he delivered her over to the warming fire, he'd hitch the other three mules together and swim them across, then return to work with the Indians floating the two wagons over the river.

He'd probably have to thaw out by the fire between each crossing.

He fastened his gaze on the two mules lunging beside him, one with a silver head bobbing above the mule swimming through the water and the other with a blonde head bobbing above the near mule, her long dress billowing out on both sides, plowing through the current.

Icy water swirling around his chest

took his breath away.

Jenny stumbled, slipped, and started floating sideways, Ben grasped Jenny's reins so hard, the leather bit into his fingers. He grabbed Felicity's arm.

She gasped. Her hazel eyes widened, and she screamed.

CHAPTER 13

As Jenny, her short tail wafting on the water behind her, Felicity clinging to her back, floated downstream toward the rapids, Jed's mule stumbled. Jed slid into the bone-chilling water, and his mule strained forward toward the bank. Jenny and Felicity swept downstream and out of Ben's reach.

Ben grasped Jed by the collar of his jacket and pulled him halfway onto Jake.

"Never mind me! Go for Felly!" Jed gasped and pushed himself off the mule. "I can swim the rest of the way."

Ben turned Jake's head downstream and kicked the big mule in the sides. Jake caught sight of his mate, Jenny, being carried downstream by the current and pricked his long ears toward her. He needed no more urging.

The big mule swam hard toward where Felicity grasped both arms around Jenny's neck. She managed to stay astride the struggling mule. Both must have been dunked underwater because Felicity's hair hung wet and stringy, and she'd lost her sun bonnet.

He and Jake caught up with Felicity. Her head lay against Jenny's neck but the rest of her body dragged beneath the swirling brown water.

A cold hand squeezed his heart. Could he save both Felicity and the mule? She'd pasted herself to the mule's back. *God, please help her retain her hold.*

He urged Jake to swim downstream until they worked their way to Felicity's side. Her wide hazel eyes showed white. Water dripped from her hair and face, and her open mouth gasped for air. She looked half drowned, but she clung to the mule's slick neck, hands intertwined in Jenny's short mane.

Ben directed Jake to push against Jenny's side and turn her toward shore. The big mule seemed to understand. He pressed his weight against Jenny. Ben's and Felicity's legs mashed together between the mules, but Jake made progress in halting Jenny's flight downstream. Both mules struggled toward shore.

As they reached more shallow water and the mules' hooves touched ground, Felicity's hands loosened. She swayed.

He dropped Jake's reins and slipped his arms around Felicity's waist. She slid off Jenny's back and would have gone under water, but he used every ounce of strength he had and pulled her in front of him onto Jake. The mule grunted but pumped his legs until his hooves touched bottom, and he scrambled up the steep mud bank.

Felicity lay against him, eyes closed, body shaking. He directed Jake toward the huge bonfire, and Jenny trotted behind her mate.

"Ben."

He leaned his head down and almost missed what she said, her teeth chattered so.

"I … I … will go … to … to California … with … you."

CHAPTER 14

The crossing had been tougher than Ben expected. He hunched on a log shivering by the fire as Jed paid the Indians who had helped. After Felicity's narrow escape, he'd wrapped her in a blanket and carried her close to the fire. The first settlers across brought her a hot cup of coffee they'd brewed.

With the sun starting its descent in the west, he'd not taken time to warm himself. He'd plunged back into the Snake River, crossed over on a mule one of the other families offered, and swam his remaining three mules, tied together head to tail, across. He'd tethered them where Jake and Jenny each rested on three hooves, Jake's head hanging over Jenny's bowed neck.

Then he'd warmed himself at the fire a few minutes.

"I'll bring that second wagon over." Jed stood from where he'd been sitting beside Felicity.

His hands trembled and he'd lost his Stetson.

"Better you stay here and look after Felicity. Make sure she doesn't take a chill." The old man sure didn't look like he could manage another crossing.

"I'll stay, but I'm dressing those quail you bagged last night. They'll taste mighty good tonight."

"Good idea. Roast quail is just what we need." Ben descended back into water so cold his bones ached. He had to float the first wagon across before the sun set.

With paid Indian help, he finally managed to float both wagons across. Drained and shivering, he straddled the log beside Felicity and Jed, warming his shivering body at the bonfire. The golden sun touched the horizon in a blaze of reds and oranges.

"Made it across just in time. Rest of the wagons will have to wait until tomorrow." Hot coffee warmed his insides, and soon Felicity, with Jed's help, would serve them all a nourishing supper.

She looked pale, but dry and competent as she turned the spit to brown the roasting quail. Aromas from the campfire set his mouth to watering. His drying clothes smelled like wet dog, and his stomach growled. He twisted around on the log to warm his back.

He should be happy. And he was. But mostly grateful. They'd crossed the most dangerous spot on the trail west, and they'd carted all Felicity's goods safely.

Felicity had promised to go southwest with him to California. He'd stake his claim and make enough money to pay off Mother's debt. Then if Felicity still wanted, he'd journey with her to the Oregon Territory.

But he had to face the gnawing doubt that grew inside his mind with each passing day. What if he didn't strike gold? What if he took Felicity into a crude mining town only to file a claim for a stake that held no gold? What if he bought a dud? Then there was the added expense of mining tools, and supplies. In the back of the wagon, Felicity's burlap bag of beans sagged only half-full. What if he'd have to resupply their food? How could he do that? Everything he owned, she'd purchased.

He owed her everything.

He'd never visited a mining town. Maybe Felicity was right. Maybe the town was too rough for a good woman.

He had to consider his wife and her needs, not merely his own problems. He frowned and dropped his head into his hands. Women had so many needs. They wanted a home. And permanence. They needed to be protected. And loved.

Oh, he loved her all right. Lot of good that did him.

Seeing her carried down the river and thinking he'd lost her had been the worst moment of his life. Yeah, he loved her.

Would she ever love him?

CHAPTER 15

Felicity stirred the beans she'd soaked in a covered pot all day in the wagon, and then placed the kettle over the campfire. She rotated the spit with the beautiful quail turning a lovely shade of golden brown. How normal everything was. How peaceful. How full of life and living.

She'd almost died.

She owed her life to Ben. Dear Ben. In the instant his arms wrapped around her and pulled her against his broad chest, she'd realized she loved him. And she had for some time.

Probably ever since that kiss.

So, tomorrow morning she and Jed would turn their wagons south, taking the fork to California. What would a mining camp be like? Would the town be as raw and bawdy as she'd heard? Surely not. Perhaps other women followed their husbands to the gold rush. Probably many wives worked alongside their husbands to pan gold.

She shivered and took a long gulp of hot coffee. Papa would be disappointed she'd not completed her journey to Oregon and homesteaded those six hundred forty acres of prime farmland. He'd preached that dreams were stargazing, and land was reality.

But she'd discovered a loving man fulfilled her dreams. He'd promised to love, honor, and protect her. And he kept his vow. Ben was the finest man she'd ever met. *Thank you, Father God, for bringing him into my life. Thank you that you do make dreams come true.*

Yes, she'd still love to own that lush farmland in the Oregon Territory. Yes, she'd still love to own a snug, permanent home. Yes, she still yearned for peace and serenity. But more than any of those dreams, she wanted to be with Ben. He was her husband. Where he went, she would follow. Like Ruth in the Bible, his people would be her people, his land her land. Of course, Ben didn't have any people of his own, but the rough miners would be his flock, and she would accept them as her people.

Despite her terrible fear, her husband would become her husband. Not every woman who delivered a child died like Mother had. She would trust God. Her God Who did exceedingly, abundantly above all she asked or thought. He would be with her in that California Gold Rush town.

She loved Ben and wanted to please him every way she could.

THE CHOICE

~

Ben jumped from the driver's seat and scuffed through the light snow that had started falling. Large flakes drifted down on his Stetson and shoulders, obscuring the late afternoon sun. His stiff fingers hurt as he unhitched the mules from the two wagons.

"Wagons camp." Caleb rode his sorrel toward them and waved his hat. "Wagons camp." The wagon master reined up next to where Ben led the eight mules to a patch of grass already dotted with snow. "Never reached this fork so late in the year before, but November's not too late. Tomorrow we split trails. Your two wagons will pull off at the South fork." Caleb pointed toward a distant diverging path. "Most of the rest of us will travel on northwest to the Oregon Territory." He reached out to shake Ben's hand. "I sure will miss you. You've been a help sharing your extra game to feed some of the other families."

Ben shook the offered hand and grinned. "Nope, you won't miss us at all. I aim to go on with the train to grab some of that free land in Oregon Territory. My wife wants a farmer for a husband, not a gold miner."

Felicity gazed up from where she'd been gathering the few pieces of kindling poking through the snow. Her pretty mouth gaped, and her beautiful hazel eyes, that turned his insides into mush, stared at him. A snowflake touched her pert nose and melted.

He'd wanted to surprise her, but not this way. "Excuse me," he said to Caleb Grant." He finished hobbling the last mule and headed toward the rear of Felicity's wagon.

He skirted the back of the wagon and looped his wife in his arms. Slowly he lowered his head and tasted those luscious lips for the second time. With a soft swish, her sunbonnet fell into the snow, and golden hair cascaded down her back.

She kissed him back. Thoroughly. And melted into his arms. Her hands wound around his neck, and her lips responded in a way that weakened his knees.

With his mouth still discovering the joy of her lips, he caressed the silky strands of her glorious hair.

Sure, he still loved adventure. But he held adventure in his arms. She was as much excitement as he could handle. Maybe more.

Sure, he loved to preach. But with his lips melded on hers and hers responding with secrets he hadn't imagined, he'd found his calling. Her body in his embrace answered warm and sweet, giving as much love as he could ever desire.

When he raised his lips, her cheeks bloomed, and her eyes sparkled. He would keep that sparkle in her eyes, no matter what it cost.

"I'll build that permanent home and

farm those hundreds of acres. I'll preach to those farmers like they'd never been preached to." He gazed into the gold caramel of her laughing eyes. "So long as you remain at my side."

"I'll never leave you."

"Somehow I'll pay off Mother's medical debt. With you at my side, I can do anything. My labor will not be in vain in the Lord."

She gazed up at him, those beautiful coppery eyes clear and brimming with admiration. "Ben, I love you. Let's celebrate an early Christmas. Will you sleep inside the wagon tonight with me?"

A lump jumped into Ben's throat. He swallowed hard. She loved him! She wanted him. His heart thundered like a herd of buffalo plowed through, forever altering the rhythm. Every shred of fatigue dissolved. He could jump over the silver moon rising in the dark sky.

Christmas had arrived three weeks

early. The best he'd ever anticipated. *Thank you, Father God.*

He kissed her again, long and slow and filled with the pent-up yearning of the last few months. He didn't even need the mistletoe he'd climbed the tree to pluck late this afternoon while snowflakes silently fell. When he lifted his head, he gazed at her captivating face, flushed and beaming, and held the mistletoe over her head. "Guess I won't need this."

She reached up, took the mistletoe, and cradled the greenery in her open palm. "No, you won't need this, but bringing this symbol to me was such a sweet thought. I'll save this to put over the doorpost of our new home." She tucked the mistletoe into the pocket of her skirt. Her laugh twinkled out. "Though I don't think *we* will need mistletoe." She stood on her tiptoes and kissed him thoroughly, then breathed a contented sigh. "I'll brew that hot mulled cider I've been saving for Christmas. We'll sip a warm toddy before we go to bed."

"Merry Christmas." Ben cupped her face in both his hands and kissed her lightly on the tip of her nose. Then on her ear lobes. Then the corner of her mouth.

"Silent night, holy night, all is calm all is bright." The song drifted from the wagon ahead where the twin sisters sang to celebrate the soon arrival of Christmas and the end of their two-thousand-mile journey.

"We've just begun our journey together as man and wife," Felicity whispered. "Love is worth waiting for, don't you think?"

He'd waited a long time. "You're right. I'd not have had our journey begin any other way." Now that he knew how precious she was, he had a new priority in his life. God, Felicity, and then preaching.

Was that only a cow bell ringing, or the chimes of Christmas day?

A silver moon in the darkened sky cast shimmering diamonds on the new fallen snow.

The twins in the wagon ahead of them sang, "Joy to the world. The Lord is come."

The scent of cloves and nutmeg in simmering mulled cider combined with the odor of pine wood burning over the campfire. He inhaled deeply.

He'd always remember that scent and this night. Christmas was God's gift to the world.

Thank you, Father, for the gift of your Son. I've learned it's so much more blessed to give than receive.

"Thank you, Felicity. Thank you for this shining moment in our lives."

"Yes," she murmured. "And we have our very own Christmas angel. God sent him to bring us together."

Dear Reader,

I hope you enjoyed **THE CHOICE** as much as I loved writing about Felicity and Ben. I'm certain you will love my other stories.

I find it such a pleasure to speak with my readers. Please visit with me at www.AnneGreeneAuthor.com, and www.facebook.com/AnneWGreeneAuthor. You can also subscribe to my newsletter so we can keep in touch. I enjoy discovering what you think about my books.

Thank you for reading THE CHOICE. Consider telling your friends or posting a short review on Amazon or Good Reads. Word of mouth is an author's best friend, and much appreciated.

ANNE GREENE delights in writing about alpha heroes who aren't afraid to fall on their knees in prayer, and about gutsy heroines. Read her latest release, *Shadow of the Dagger.* Enjoy her *Women of Courage series* which spotlights heroic women of World War II, first book *Angel With Steel Wings.* Read her *Holly Garden Private Investigating series, Handcuffed In Texas,* first book *Red Is For Rookie.* Enjoy her award-winning Scottish historical romances, *Masquerade Marriage* and *Marriage By Arrangement.* Anne's highest hope is that her stories transport you to an awesome new world and touch your heart to seek a deeper spiritual relationship with the Lord Jesus.

Visit with Anne at
www.AnneGreeneAuthor.com
www.facebook.com/AnneWGreeneAuthor
LINKS TO BUY ANNE'S

BOOKS:

If you're an electronic reader, click on the following links to learn about Anne's other books. If you are a print book reader, you will find all her books listed on my website, http://www.AnneGreeneAuthor.com or on https://www.amazon.com/Anne-Greene/e/B004ECUWMG

> Hatteras Island Mystery
> Shadow of the Dagger
> Angel with Steel Wings
> Holly Garden, PI: Red Is for Rookie
> Masquerade Marriage
> Marriage By Arrangement
> A Texas Christmas Mystery
> A Christmas Belle
> The California Gold Rush Romance Collection: 9 Stories of Finding Treasures Worth   More than Gold – The Marriage Broker and the Mortician
> Keara's Escape (A Spinster Orphan Train novella)

Daredevils

- Daredevils
- Spur of the Moment Bride
- A Groom for Christmas
- Avoiding the Mistletoe
- A Rebel Spy
- Lord Bentley Needs A Bride
- Mystery at Dead Broke Ranch
- Her Reluctant Hero
- A Crazy Optimist
- Texas Law
- Recipe For A Husband
- A Williamsburg Christmas
- Anne Greene Author Home Page
- Anne Greene's Books on Amazon

ENJOY CHAPTER ONE OF ANNE'S BOOK, HATTERAS ISLAND MYSTERY

CHAPTER 1

Misty Gordon dug her toes into the cool sand to steady the shot. Sunrays filtered through the light fog and touched her arms with gold.

She adjusted her camera until she captured the bride and groom with the Cape Hatteras Lighthouse in the background.

She finished the photo array with a view of the couple in front of the expanse of the Atlantic Ocean. This early morning series marked her as unique among the photographers on the island.

She bid good-bye to the bride and groom, stowed her camera in its bag, and took off across the sand to clear her thoughts.

Her business, Lighthouse Photography, made a comfortable living, and she loved her town, Hatteras, located on the Outer Banks of North Carolina, especially in December when most tourists had long departed.

Though she also offered an amazing portfolio of landscapes and portraits, most of her pictorial art revolved around weddings. She enjoyed photographing brides in flowing white gowns coupled with smiling grooms sporting tuxes. Her most popular pose featured the groom's hand cupping the bride's chin, kissing her, the wind nestling her long gown around his legs, his polished wingtips and her spiked heels sinking into the sand with the sparkling Atlantic as their background.

Each bride and groom Misty photographed started their journey of life together expecting a happily-ever-after lifetime. Misty, a born romantic, did her utmost to record their happiness with her photographs.

Until last summer, when taking posed and candid shots of love-in-bloom had become bittersweet. The last of her three best friends had tread the sand aisle behind the most beautiful church on the island.

As life-long friends, since their teens, she and her three besties had planned weddings-to-die-for on the sands of the Outer Banks as the sun rose in a glorious blaze of color over the Atlantic. She'd been thrilled to photograph each one's wedding as each friend saw her dream blossom into reality. But she, Misty Gordon, was the last bridesmaid standing.

Misty frowned and wrinkled her nose. She wasn't getting any younger. But the men in her photos were.

With December's arrival, Christmas in Hatteras threatened yet another sparse-in-the-single-male-department. She could look forward to fighting a bout of the holiday blues.

That pending holiday probably explained why at the last wedding she'd photographed, she'd snapped so many digital pictures of the one man in the Hamiltons' wedding who appeared to be single. Misty kicked her bare toes at the firm wet sand along the water's edge. Why hadn't she asked the unattached male his name?

She'd always been a sucker for a man with a beard. The stranger's dark hair and beard framed an attractive face, neither too handsome nor too rugged. Quite a photogenic face…with a tall, athletic body to showcase the fine head. If she'd obtained a release, she might have sold his pictures to one of the men's clothing businesses and made a bundle. The man was a natural model with his relaxed manner and easy smile. She could have offered him that new career. And learned his name.

But the dreamy guy exited the wedding before she could ask him to sign a photography release. Her rainbow disappeared from arching over her pot of gold. She'd failed to get his name.

When the Hamiltons viewed their album, the new Mr. and Mrs. hadn't appreciated her photographic pictorial of their wedding journey. They'd wanted more pictures of themselves and claimed the man wasn't a close family member, and they didn't appreciate so many shots of him.

She only taken four shots of the GQ man, but she'd returned the deposit money to her first dissatisfied customers. Even then, the couple refused to reveal the GQ model's name. If he lived on Hatteras, he wasn't a celebrity, but her label for the stranger stuck in her mind.

That day, she'd gone so far as to haunt the Hatteras Coast Guard substation sector field office, pretending to take pictures for an imaginary magazine, but hadn't seen the extra-broad shoulders, tall athletic form, nor his easy-on-the-eyes features.

She should have realized the Coast Guard didn't accept beards. The guys stationed there all wore dark blue, short-sleeved uniforms with their name ribbons on the right side of their chests and the Coast Guard ribbon on the left. Some had looked appealing but worn already-taken-rings on their left-hand finger. She'd never appreciated a military haircut anyway. She liked abundant locks on a man's head.

She gazed at the waves rolling and frothing on the sand. Her thoughts weren't clearing. Nevertheless, she bent, dug up a perfect sand dollar and flicked off the clinging sand. Brides adored their invitations photographed with these delicate shells, so this morning she could replenish her stock.

The risen sun painted the stark white shell pink, much like her rosy romantic dreams had been. She heaved a deep sigh. Naïve to think she could re-start a new life in Hatteras. Find a new love, one who wouldn't betray her. Of course, the years had sped by, and she hadn't. In her field of work, she met only already-spoken-for bachelors. Would her time to walk the aisle ever come?

Cool water washed over her feet. She slung her camera bag over her shoulder.

Something bumped her ankle. She jumped. Her breath drained from her lungs.

Something large. Heavens, a body! Flat on his back, hair plastered over his face, navy slacks shredded, a ripped white long-sleeved shirt clung to his torso, feet bare, a man floated in the surf. Pushed one way and then another, the body undulated with the waves. She touched the wet shoulder.

His eyes were closed, but the slight rise and fall of his chest showed he was alive.

She reached into her pocket, pulled out her cell and dialed 911.

"Come on, answer, answer!" How much longer would this man breathe?

She knelt in the surf beside him, her knees sinking into the shifting sand, the sun warming her back, strands of her long, blond hair blowing into her eyes as she touched his carotid artery.

A stammering pulse beat erratic, but strong.

He looked to be in top physical shape. Had he been washed off a fishing vessel? Sand-matted dark hair plastered his forehead. A purple bruise marred his left temple and spread below his eye. A crease between his dark, straight brows showed the pain he must have endured when whatever injured him had hurled him into the sea.

She glanced out at Diamond Shoals, known for years as the Graveyard of the Atlantic. No wrecked vessel.

Normally she charged into situations before she considered the consequences. But this breathtakingly handsome man, rocking in the surf at her feet, left her panting like a tourist trying to climb the lighthouse stairs. She glanced up. "Where is that medical help? I can't let this man to die."

His limp fingers bobbed in the water, long and graceful and empty of rings.

Shame on her for thinking of his marital status at a time like this.

She grasped his shoulders and tugged and strained until she dragged him out of the cool water and up onto dry sand. Beneath his tattered shirt, his skin felt cold.

A siren in the distance shrilled louder. She turned. "Hurry! Hurry! Hurry!" She spun back toward the unconscious man and plunked in the sand beside him. Why hadn't she learned CPR?

His eyes were open. Dark but blank.

She half-lifted him and turned his torso to the side. "Cough! Breathe! Sputter! Anything!" She bent him over and pounded his back.

He choked, his shoulders heaved, and water spurted from his mouth.

He looked familiar. Where had she seen him? She shook her head. He was a stranger.

"Where am I?" His voice sounded strangled, weak.

She massaged his back. "Near the Hatteras Lighthouse. What happened to you?"

He leaned against her, his upper body, wet, heavy and chilled. He moved his hand to his forehead and blinked. "Who are you?"

The sirens squealed louder and louder.

"I found you. What happened to you?"

He frowned. Shaded his eyes with his hand. "I don't know." His words slurred, and he coughed.

Paramedics ran toward them. One carried a stretcher, the other a large white bag.

"Were you fishing? Sailing?" She helped him sit up.

He blinked and rubbed his eyes with both fists. "I don't know."

One paramedic knelt beside her. The second ran to the injured man's other side, his shoes spraying globs of sand and water over her. "What's your name?"

The man shook his head, ruffling the sand from his hair like water shaken from a dog. He blinked and kneaded his eyes with his fingers.

The paramedic gazed across the stricken man at her. "What's his name?"

"I have no idea. I found him here. Like this." She dug her camera out of her bag.

The first responder leaned over the man. "How many fingers do you see?" He held up three.

"Three."

Misty snapped his picture.

"Give me your name, sir."

"I...I don't remember."

Made in the USA
Coppell, TX
29 May 2024

32925703R00099